BONE
HOLLOW

BONE HOLLOW

· KIM VENTRELLA ·

SCHOLASTIC PRESS · NEW YORK

All rights reserved. Published by Scholastic Press, an imprint of Scholastic Inc., *Publishers since 1920*. SCHOLASTIC, SCHOLASTIC PRESS, and associated logos are trademarks and/or registered trademarks of Scholastic Inc.

The publisher does not have any control over and does not assume any responsibility for author or third-party websites or their content.

Library of Congress Cataloging-in-Publication Data available

ISBN 978-1-338-04274-0

10 9 8 7 6 5 4 3 2 1   19 20 21 22 23

Printed in the U.S.A.   23
First edition, March 2019
Book design by Yaffa Jaskoll

To Hera

BONE
HOLLOW

CHAPTER ONE
· THE STORM ·

A tornado touched down in Macomb County at the same time Gabe climbed to the top of Miss Cleo's roof in search of a chicken. To be fair, nobody knew where that tornado was headed till it was far too late. And besides, it's not like Miss Cleo sent him up there in search of just any ordinary barnyard hen. It was Princess Carmella, Miss Cleo's prize Sicilian Buttercup, winner of the Canadian Valley Poultry Expo three years running.

"Watch out for the tail feathers," Miss Cleo said, clutching Princess Carmella's favorite blanket to her chest.

Soon, the neighbors wandered over to investigate, and Miss Cleo put them to work tossing every pillow they could find across the yard in hopes of a softer landing.

Of course, none of that would be necessary if Gabe did his job.

"Do you see her?" called Mr. Lawson, owner of Lawson's New and Used Hardware. He was by far the tallest of the bunch, and standing on his tiptoes he could just make out the figure of a boy crawling across the roof. "Don't spook her, now. Nice and slow."

"And quiet!" shouted Miss Cleo at the top of her voice.

So Gabe crept, slow and quiet, across Miss Cleo's roof, which was his roof, too, it should be pointed out, though maybe not for long. The tiles sagged in spots, where the rainwater had gotten in. If he pressed down too hard, they started to creak and crack under his weight, and so he moved like Mr. Lawson's old cat. Ghost was a giant cat, the color of ash, but he flew over the packed shelves of the hardware store with such skill and finesse he really might have been a ghost, or at least that's what people said.

Down below, Gabe's trusty dog, and best friend, Ollie, barked in a panic. Gabe didn't speak dog, but he had a pretty good idea he was saying, "Get down from there right now—storm's a-coming!"

If only it were that easy. Miss Cleo was real nice, letting Gabe and Ollie stay with her after his parents passed, but he didn't stay for free. He had to "put in the work," the way she told it, and most of that work involved looking after Princess Carmella. That dang chicken was more like family to Miss Cleo than he'd ever been.

And, just like that, Gabe spotted her, perched atop the chimney, preening her dumb speckled feathers.

"There you are, you mangy old hen," Gabe said, though not loud enough for anyone down below to hear. Miss Cleo did not take kindly to anyone insulting her prize poultry. Like the time he'd accidentally sat on Princess Carmella, on account of her being tucked surreptitiously into his very own bed. Despite the fact that he hadn't been to blame, seeing as it was his bed and nobody had warned him there might be a chicken inside, Miss Cleo had given him a whupping he wouldn't soon forget.

"Gosh dangit!" Gabe added as a raindrop the size of a hummingbird plopped onto his head. That raindrop was followed by another and another, each one bigger than the last.

"Hurry up!" cried Miss Cleo. "That storm'll be here in a tick. You know what happens when Princess Carmella gets wet."

What happened was that Miss Cleo would spend the whole night cradling that hen in her favorite velvety blanket, the one with her name embroidered on the back. Then, in the morning, her feathers would be one big ball of frizz. "Gosh dang chicken!"

A bolt of lightning lit up the clouds, just like in the movies, and Princess Carmella released an ear-pinching squawk. She leapt off the chimney with ease, landing on the tip of the iron weather vane, which had been hewn in her very own image. Her beady black eyes met his just as another bolt of lightning streaked overhead. Her eyes flashed yellow, and Gabe swore that if chickens could talk she'd be laughing at him.

"Got you now," Gabe said.

The pounding rain drowned out all the voices down below,

so it was just him and the chicken. And Ollie, straining to be heard over all that wind. That dog was awful terrified of storms, and Gabe would be glad when he could get down off this roof and comfort him. Poor, wimpy hound.

"I've had enough!" Gabe said, partly to rev himself up, partly to put the fear of God into that good-for-nothing chicken.

In a burst of energy, he scrambled up the arched roof, his sneakers squeaking on the wet tile. "You're mine!" Gabe lunged, grabbing for a wing or a foot or a whatever he could get ahold of. He no longer cared about ruffling feathers.

His fingers grazed the edge of a wrinkly toe, but at the last minute Princess Carmella leapt into the air. She landed a few feet away, shaking her speckled tail feathers right in his face.

That was when he heard Mr. Lawson shouting something from down below. At first, he couldn't quite make out the word he was saying, over and over, like a prayer. The wind was so wild and the rain so fierce, it was all he could do to hang on to that weather vane for dear life.

Then a gust of wind swooped down and scooped up Princess Carmella, like a giant hand reaching out of the sky. She flew up and up and up into the towering gray clouds, right along with his chances of ever setting foot in Miss Cleo's house again, and that was when Gabe understood the word Mr. Lawson was shouting.

"Twister!"

Gabe tightened his grip on the weather vane. He felt mighty bad for what had happened to Princess Carmella, but he wasn't about to let the same thing happen to him. He had a dog down below who was depending on him, and if he flew away, he could be dang sure Miss Cleo wouldn't take care of Ollie. She'd never had any love to spare for dogs, or for him, when it came right down to it.

"I'm coming, Ollie!" he shouted, sucking down a mouthful of rain. He folded his arms tight as can be around that wrought iron chicken and started to pray.

"Please, please, please, please," he said, "don't let me die on account of a chicken." Though he really did feel bad for her. "Tell Ollie not to be scared, Lord, if you're up there. Please, please, please."

As if in answer to his prayer, the wind went still for a moment and the black sky lit up, glowing a dirty shade of gold. *Thank all the chickens in the world*, Gabe thought. *From this day forward I'll never curse another chicken.* But then a swirling funnel of wind dropped down out of the clouds.

It picked up a telephone pole as if it were light as a splinter and tossed it at the Bentons' farm. The roof underneath him started to shake. The tornado whined as it cut a path across the town.

"I've got to get off this roof," Gabe thought out loud, but then a gust of wind picked him up and carried him high into the air. Time froze for a while, as Gabe realized he still had hold of that weather vane, though it was no longer attached to the roof. He could hear Ollie, whimpering down below, a note of true desperation in his voice.

Then, faster than Mr. Lawson's cat, Ghost, the whole world sped by, and Gabe hit the ground hard with a crack!

———

Green bean casserole was the first thing Gabe smelled when he woke up. He was lying in Miss Cleo's very own bed. Which was strange, because that was one of the many places he wasn't allowed. He could tell it was her bed because along with the scent of creamy casserole was the not-so-pleasant aroma of Miss Cleo's homemade toe gel. It was a mixture of Vaseline and fresh egg yolk. In short, it stunk.

Stranger still, his loyal dog, Ollie, was curled up at his side, resting his long, skinny nose on his chest. If it was strange for Miss Cleo to let him sleep in her bed, it was unheard of for her to let Ollie in the house, let alone on her thousand-dollar, Sleep-o-matic mattress.

"What a brave boy," Miss Cleo was saying, pulling a Kleenex out from her bra. "He looks just like he's sleeping, doesn't he? I always said he had a kind heart, didn't I? But who knew he'd face down a twister to save my sweet princess?"

To Gabe's astonishment, Ethylene Roberts, who used to babysit Gabe when he was little, despite not being much older than him, walked into the room carrying a familiar ball of reddish-brown frizz. It was Princess Carmella, a little rumpled but none the worse for wear.

"Oh, just look at the state of you!" Miss Cleo said, wrapping the chicken in her velvety blanket, the one with her name sewn on the back. "And aren't you the bravest of all, for surviving such a storm?"

Miss Cleo buried her head in the chicken's fluffy feathers, and to Gabe's further surprise, Princess Carmella turned one black marble eye on him and winked. Or maybe he imagined it. Either way, Ollie started barking something awful, probably trying to defend him, and Gabe decided it was time to give that chicken a piece of his mind. After all, she'd been the cause of this whole dang debacle.

He tried to sit up, but he was covered in each and every one of Miss Cleo's hand-knitted blankets, the ones she bought every year at the Ladies of the Bible charity auction.

"If you don't mind, Miss Cleo, I'd like a quick word with your bird. And it's not going to be a nice one, either, I'm sorry to say." It was always better to warn Miss Cleo before cursing or otherwise misbehaving. To Gabe's annoyance, she didn't answer or even look up.

"Taken from us too soon," Miss Cleo was going on, as a few more neighbors poured into the small room, hanging on her every word. "That's what they would have said about you, isn't it, sweetie pie?" She kissed Princess Carmella right on the beak, not once but three or four times. "Thank goodness there was a hero on hand to save you."

"Bless his soul," said Mrs. Romero, Gabe's sixth-grade teacher, dabbing tears from her eyes.

Mr. Lawson brought around a Kleenex box and everybody grabbed at least one or two, even if they weren't near to crying.

"What about me?" Gabe said, not that he planned to tear up over some misbehaving chicken, but still. Maybe he was a little bit happy she was okay, and who knows, maybe he needed to blow his nose.

Nobody answered, not even his best friend Chance, who walked in carrying a pizza box from Penny's Sweet and Savory Pies. Gabe could tell just by the smell that it was his and Chance's favorite, double jalapeño with pepperoni on the side.

"Nice," Gabe said. "I'm starving."

Chance pretended not to hear him. Not only that, but he wouldn't even come all the way into the room. He kept sniffling and staring at his shoes, like maybe they were stuffed full of ragweed.

"Seriously, it's not like I didn't try to save your dumb old hen," Gabe said, frustration heating up his words. "I'd like to see one of you all climb up to the roof in the middle of a thunderstorm, all on account of some spoiled rotten chicken." Honestly, there he was, trying to do something nice, and just maybe get on Miss Cleo's good side, and how'd he get repaid? With a cold shoulder big enough to freeze Texas, that's how!

Ollie nuzzled Gabe's neck and licked his chin. At least he understood. But it was strange, because Gabe could see Ollie licking and nuzzling, but he couldn't feel a thing. Almost as if he was watching the whole scene from outside his own body, like some kind of ghost.

Meanwhile, Ethylene blubbered into her Kleenex, though Gabe didn't think it was because of his words. "We used to play Super Mario every day after school. I always let him win. And now . . ."

She tried to keep going, but tears clogged out the rest of her words. That was fine by Gabe, because he'd heard enough. No way she'd let him win. In fact, she'd only gotten past the first level once, and that was because she'd stolen his controller just before the end.

Ethylene filed out, and so did Mr. Lawson and little Danny Romero, clinging to his mama's arm. Chance left, too, taking the steaming hot pizza with him. Some of the neighbors leaned over Gabe's bed before they left, blowing big globs of snot into their Kleenexes.

"Goodbye, champ," said Mr. Peters, Gabe's track coach at Macomb Junior High.

"Poor kid," said Chip Evans, the voice of Macomb County's only radio station, 107.3 Hip FM.

Miss Cleo was the last to go, sitting down on the edge of the bed. She took the unprecedented step of putting Princess Carmella on the ground instead of in her lap, which shocked

Gabe more than just about anything. Miss Cleo stared at him for a long, long time, the dim lamplight reflecting off her watery eyes.

"We didn't always get along, you and I. But I took care of you after your mama and daddy died, and you was a good boy." She stopped and her face twisted up, like she was about to let loose a whole bunch of tears.

"It's okay," Gabe said, though he still had no idea what on earth was happening.

After doing some of her relaxation breathing, Miss Cleo continued, "A real good boy, I hope you know that. Wherever you are." With that, she bent down to kiss him on the forehead, and that was when Ollie did something so out of character, Gabe gasped.

He snarled and snapped the air right next to Miss Cleo's face.

Shaken, Miss Cleo backed away from the bed. She muttered something under her breath that sounded like "poor mutt," and then she scooped up her chicken and went out of the room, shutting the door softly behind her.

Gabe was alone. Well, not really alone. Ollie settled down with his head resting protectively on Gabe's stomach.

"Everybody sure has been acting funny today," Gabe said. Then again, funny was what most folks around here did best.

"Help me get out from under these covers," Gabe instructed, and Ollie, being a good dog, obliged.

At first, Gabe still couldn't move his legs, like he was looking at his own body from the outside. Then he closed his eyes
and concentrated hard. Ollie licked his face by way of encouragement, and soon he felt that big, wet tongue slobbering
his skin. Thank goodness! Gabe was too young to be a ghost.
Together, they tugged and pulled and pushed until Gabe was
able to slide his legs out from under the heap of blankets.

"Now, that doesn't look right," Gabe said, staring down at
something altogether unusual in the middle of his bare stomach.

He was about to try and figure out what it was when the
door banged open and a stranger came in. A black hood hung
low over his eyes, and he smelled an awful lot like worms.

CHAPTER TWO

• CAPTAIN •

It was as if someone had sucked all the light from the room
and the only thing Gabe could see was a hulking figure silhou-
etted in the doorway. He wore a long black cloak, but it wasn't
the kind you could buy at Pierson Drug right around Halloween.
It was a real cloak made of fancy velvet, and it wasn't just black,
either. It was the color of midnight if you were way out down
some country road on a starless, moonless night.

Ollie growled low and deep, a growl that should have been
reserved for some wild jungle beast. He sank into a crouch, like
he was readying himself to spring, and every black and brown
hair stood up in a three-inch-tall mohawk down his back.

And this was the same dog who usually hid from houseflies
and once let an escaped kitten named Prancer chase him across
the Bentons' farm. Gabe would have chided him for forgetting
his good manners, but he figured he might have growled, too,
if he'd been a dog. He didn't like the way the stranger's hood
rippled, like it was caught up in an invisible wind.

"Who are you?" Gabe said.

It dawned on him that it might be Elmer from the Pump 'n' Save playing a practical joke. He did have a tendency to jump out from behind the gas station counter wearing a Darth Vader mask and scaring Gabe's classmates silly. But it also struck him that Elmer had never once been to his house, and he nearly always broke out laughing halfway through trying to hide.

"This isn't funny," Gabe said, but before the words had left his mouth, Ollie lunged. Gabe tried to grab him, but the dog was too fast. He collided with the stranger and sank his jaws into that cloak, tearing it clean from the stranger's head.

Gabe couldn't have been more shocked if he'd tried, because the stranger wasn't Elmer or an axe-wielding murderer or anybody he could have expected. It was his very own gramps.

"Sorry to frighten you," Gramps said, coming to lean over Gabe's bed. Gabe blinked, expecting Gramps to fade away like the ghost he was, but boy, did he look solid. Even stranger, he seemed to shrink before Gabe's eyes, until he was no longer tall and scary but a thin, wiry old man, just like Gabe remembered. He wore a powder-blue polo shirt with navy-blue pants, and he smelled just like a fresh-cut lawn. At the sight of him, all the fight drained out of that fearsome dog, and he turned his attention to wiggling his bottom.

"That scratch on your tummy's not lookin' too good," Gramps said.

Gabe peered down at his stomach. In all the chaos, he'd totally forgotten about what he'd seen there. It wasn't a scratch, like Gramps said. It was a hole. Like someone had gone in and dug out a new belly button right next to his old one. Only there was something he didn't like about this new belly button, not one little bit.

Gramps smiled, that sad half smile he used when he was getting around to sharing bad news. "How's your back feeling, Captain?" Gramps always called him Captain, on account of him jumping off the shed when he was six and trying to fly.

"Fine," Gabe said.

"Have a look."

He had no clue what Gramps was on about. Gramps was the one with a bad back, not him. Still, he did some feeling around back there just to satisfy him.

"There's nothing, Gramps. I'm fit as a fiddle."

"Check again."

So he did a little more feeling around, and this time Ollie came to help him. He found nothing at first, until he felt a tongue slip in somewhere it shouldn't have.

"What on earth!" Gabe said.

Ollie licked the same spot again, and that was when Gabe found it. A hole, just like the one in his stomach. He poked his finger in, and then shivered. It wasn't like a belly button at all. The inside was wet and sticky.

"What is it?" Gabe said. "What's happened to me?"

Gramps didn't say anything for a good long while.

"This is because of that dang chicken, isn't it?" Gabe said. And because of Miss Cleo, for sending him up on that roof in the middle of a thunderstorm. If only he could've lived with Gramps after his parents died, instead of her, this never would've happened. It was all Miss Cleo's fault. And maybe Gramps's fault, too, for going off and leaving him.

Gramps still didn't answer. He leaned down like he meant to kiss Gabe right on the forehead. The room around them grew fuzzy and started to spin.

"What's happening?" Gabe said.

"Time to go."

"Where to?"

"You'll see."

Gramps didn't kiss Gabe, though. He stopped short, a confused expression on his face. His eyes looked strange up close, like a roiling thunderstorm struck through with light.

"What's the matter, Gramps? Where are we going?"

Gramps stood up straight again, a frown etched deep on his wrinkled face.

"Is something wrong?" Gabe said, but it was as if Gramps couldn't hear him.

Without another word, he picked up his cloak from where it had fallen on the ground and walked away. He stopped just inside the doorway, ignoring Ollie, who was trying to play a game of "herd the sheep" with his heels.

"I'm mighty sorry about all this, Captain."

Then, despite Ollie's best efforts, he was gone.

CHAPTER THREE

· HOMECOMING ·

Gabe would have gone after Gramps, had he not suddenly felt more exhausted than he had in his whole entire life. He sank down into Miss Cleo's toe cream–scented pillows and fell into a deep sleep, Ollie keeping watch at his side.

He had no idea how long he slept, but it must have been a good long while, because he woke up in a room he didn't recognize. No more thousand-dollar mattress, or flowery toe cream sheets. Just a cold metal table like they had in the kitchens at Dena's Family Diner. And, horror upon horrors, there was Gabe lying on that table naked as the day he was born.

The first thing he did was leap to the tile and search around for something to cover up with. There wasn't much in that room at all, apart from tall metal cabinets and a long, stainless steel countertop. Not a sheet or a napkin or a single scrap of fabric to be found.

He was about to give up hope when he spotted a plastic bag tied up and tossed in a corner. He had an inkling he recognized the contents. Sure enough, when he ripped it open, he found the clothes he'd been wearing just a short while before. He pulled on his underwear first, happy as pie to have it back in its proper place. Then he zipped up his jeans, stuck his feet in his shoes, and smoothed out his wrinkled T-shirt.

There was a hole clean through the center, and the edges were stained with dark brown mud. Gabe slid it over his head, and he couldn't help but notice that the holes in the T-shirt matched up exactly with the ones in his stomach and back.

For a second, he was up on that roof again, watching that dusty old finger descend from the sky. He remembered the eerie whining of it, and the crackle in the air, and the way it tore up trees as easy as plucking the legs off a cockroach. And he remembered falling, but more than anything he remembered wishing he could get down and comfort his dumb old dog. Which begged the question. What had Miss Cleo done with Ollie?

More than likely she'd kicked him out of the house to fend off the stray cats and coyotes. No way she'd have let him continue sleeping in her bed after she brought Gabe to this . . . this whatever it was. It looked like some kind of hospital. And maybe a hospital made sense, 'cause apart from his brain aching like a ball of mashed-up playdough, Gabe felt better than ever. Better than he had in his whole dang life. Like he'd swallowed a pack of wild stallions, and now they were snorting and raring inside his chest.

That had been some kind of strange dream, with him floating in the air and Gramps wearing that oversize cape, but thank goodness it was over.

"I'm gonna find my dog and demand that Miss Cleo treat him better," he said out loud, by way of convincing himself he was really gonna do it. "Ollie's a member of this family, and he stays in my room from now on, or no more free chicken rustling. Who ever heard of letting a no-good chicken sleep in the house, and not a true and loyal canine?" *And while I'm at it, maybe I'll demand that Miss Cleo start treatin' me like a real, bona fide member of the family,* he thought. He didn't dare say "like a son," even in his own head.

Gabe puffed out his chest and stood his ground, pretending like Miss Cleo was standing right there in front of him. Of course, a pretend Miss Cleo and a real Miss Cleo were two entirely different things. He decided he'd better act fast, before he lost his nerve, and that meant escaping this gosh dang hospital.

"Doc?" Gabe called, his voice echoing around the empty room. "Nurse?"

There were two doors in the room. The first one he tried was locked. He pushed through the second door easy-peasy and then covered his eyes. Sunlight blasted his face, and Gabe blinked at it in confusion. How long had he been asleep?

He was just pondering this problem through watering eyes when something wet and slobbery attacked his chin.

"Ollie, there you are!" Gabe tumbled onto the grass, and the door to the mysterious room closed behind him. He pulled Ollie into a hug and petted his soft, warm tummy. Gabe was pretty sure he'd never been so happy to see someone in his whole dang life.

Once Ollie had finally calmed down enough to stop licking his face, Gabe looked up to see that the building he'd come out of wasn't a hospital at all. He was sitting on the grass outside Morton & Sons Funeral Home. The sign closest to the street read, "Saying goodbye in style."

"What on earth?" Gabe said, shaking his head at the sign. He kept on shaking his head, giving his brain a good jostle, until he came to the only logical conclusion. Surely somebody was having a good ol' laugh at his expense. A big, fat practical joke. That's what it had to be, 'cause otherwise . . . A nasty thought wriggled at the back of his head, but he ignored it.

"Well, forget about those jokers, boy. Let's go home and get some food in your belly. Besides, we need to have a talk with Miss Cleo."

Ollie barked and wiggled his bottom in response. He knew the word "food," and it always made him happy. Gabe often thought it'd be nice to find that much happiness in a single word. His friend Niko had been the same way. She even used to make up her own words, like "scrumdumpulous" for food that you dropped on the floor, but only for a second, and "splendooferous" for when you did something dumb that ended up working out great. Hearing her words always made Gabe laugh. He wondered what she'd call it when you woke up one day and found yourself naked in a funeral home.

Too bad he couldn't ask her, since Niko had up and moved away.

"All this contemplating is giving me a headache," Gabe said to Ollie. "Come on, boy, last one there's a stinky, rotten egg!"

Gabe ran, and he had a strange feeling he was running faster than he'd ever run before. He leapt over a tall row of hedges onto Astor Street. Ollie made it, too, though just barely. Usually that mutt could outrun him easily, with his long body and powerful legs, but not so today. Gabe took a sharp left at the Pump 'n' Save, jumping the small fence and taking the shortcut across the Bentons' farm.

The fallow field was soggy from all the rain, and Gabe's sneakers soon got swallowed by the mud. Ollie ran circles around him, too light to sink. He was always excited any time he got to make a mess, like a real dog, which was pretty much never, unless he wanted Miss Cleo to turn the hose on him. Gabe looked down at the sticky brown muck oozing up past his ankles. Gosh dang.

"Guess I've got no choice," he said to Ollie. He pried his feet out of his shoes and ran over the mud barefoot, going even faster than before. So fast, the mud didn't have time to get ahold of him. So fast, someone watching from the edge of the field wouldn't be able to say for sure whether or not his feet touched the ground.

"Hurry up, slowpoke!" Gabe called as he passed Ollie and leapt over the fence into Miss Cleo's front yard. The grass was littered with dandelions and raw eggs, on account of her letting the chickens run free. Gabe did his best not to step on any of the eggs, but he couldn't avoid the occasional crunch. Ollie knew better than to try and gobble any down, as that was likely to result in Miss Cleo chasing him around the yard with her feather duster, or even worse, a switch.

Gabe busted through the front door without bothering to knock. If Miss Cleo had been home, she would have yelped and told him to come inside the right way or don't bother coming in at all.

Instead, the house was quiet.

"Miss Cleo?" Gabe said, but the only answer was the buzz of the refrigerator and the drip, drip, drip of water in the hall toilet. Gabe went to check the hen room, where Miss Cleo did all her official poultry competition business, but the lights were off. He was all ready to make his demands on Ollie's behalf, and say a few choice words about that dang chicken, but Miss Cleo was nowhere to be found.

His room was empty, too, so he decided to check the only other place she could be, Miss Cleo's very own bedroom.

The bare skin on his arms prickled as he stepped into the doorway and saw the empty bed. It was piled high with blankets, but there was a dip in the middle, as if someone had recently gotten up without bothering to make the bed. A vase of flowers stood on the nightstand and two more on the dresser.

Fuzzy images flitted into his mind piece by piece, neighbors and casseroles and sniffling noses. It had to be a dream, surely it did, but then why did everything in the room look so familiar? Ollie leapt onto Miss Cleo's bed and smiled, like it was the most natural thing in the whole wide world.

"Get on down here, you silly hound," Gabe said, but he wasn't really mad. Not like Miss Cleo's bed was all that special, no matter what she said.

Seeing as she wasn't home, he plopped down onto the mattress himself, releasing a cloud of unmistakable stink: Miss Cleo's toe cream. Gabe had read in a magazine once that smell has the best memory of any of the senses. Dang if that article didn't turn out to be true. As soon as he got a whiff of that pungent Miss Cleo stink, he remembered everything that had happened in his dream, and it wasn't the least bit fuzzy. The casseroles, all his neighbors coming by to see him, acting like he wasn't even there. Like he had gone and died or something.

The world started spinning around him at that thought, along with his memories. Miss Cleo and Chase and the others ignoring every word he said. The green bean casserole that Miss Cleo only ever made for weddings or funerals, and there wasn't nobody getting married. And Gabe, floating along outside his body, unable to move or be heard. But it couldn't be true. No way. He couldn't be . . . That is to say, surely it wasn't possible that he was . . . But no, he was still here, up and walking around. He was solid, not like any ghost he'd ever met. And he definitely wasn't . . . dead.

"No, siree," Gabe said slowly, after thinking on it a while. How could he be dead when he was still here? Still flesh and bone? There had to be some other explanation. "But what?" he said, hoping Ollie might have an answer.

In response, Ollie flipped onto his back, closed his eyes, and waited for a belly rub. "That doesn't help, you dang dog." But then again, maybe it did. Ollie wasn't much for playing dead, on account of his tail wiggling, but Gabe had once known a possum to play dead for three whole hours before leaping up and scrabbling off into the bush. Maybe that's what had happened. Only he hadn't been playing, he'd been in some kind of coma or something. One that lasted a really long time, long enough to fool all his friends and neighbors into thinking he was deceased. Why else would they have acted so strange, and then up and abandoned him? There was no other explanation. All his neighbors, even Miss Cleo, thought he was cold on a slab somewhere, waiting to be buried, but it was all some kind of mistake.

After all, nobody, not even Elmer from the Pump 'n' Save, would put a kid in a morgue just for a joke.

"They all think I'm dead!"

Gabe kissed Ollie smack-dab on the nose at the thought

of it. Not the part about being dead, but the part about his actually being alive. That kiss got Ollie really excited, and Gabe had to take a short break to rub his belly and scratch his chest. When Ollie got that excited, there was no way around it.

With the bulk of the belly rubbing satisfied, Gabe hopped out of bed, as fired up as a telephone wire in a windstorm at his new discovery. He had to find Miss Cleo and Chance and everybody else in town and pass on the great news. Not only was he not dearly departed, he felt better than he ever had. Chicken or no chicken.

First, he stopped to give Ollie his food and get him some water. Miss Cleo wouldn't spring for anything better than scraps and moldy bread, but Gabe always saved him some meat from dinner the night before. He opened up the fridge, only to find his Tupperware full of liver covered in a film of green mold.

"Yuck! How on earth did that food turn so fast?"

Instead, he fed Ollie the only other thing he could find, a heap of crusty egg-and-cheese casserole and the last slice of deli turkey.

Ollie downed it all in under a second, along with a good stomach-full of water, and with that they took off again, this time heading straight for the church.

As far as Gabe could remember, the storm had come on a Wednesday, so that meant today Miss Cleo would be at church for her Thursday lunch with Pastor Higgins and the Ladies of the Holy Ghost knitting circle/Bible study. Besides, pretty much everybody in town who wasn't learning or working made a point to stop in at church around lunchtime, since it was a well-known fact that Mrs. Higgins served up fresh-baked apple butter scones at noon sharp to any hungry souls who might happen to pass.

Racing down Main Street, Gabe was surprised to see a "Closed" sign on nearly every shop. There was only one car outside Dena's Family Diner, and it had "For Sale" written on the back window in white paint. Ollie nipped at Gabe's heels as he ran, having about as much fun as he'd ever had in his whole dang life, judging by his dopey expression.

Gabe sprinted up Very Tall Hill and into the churchyard. His bones were so itchy for a bit of exercise he leapt over three headstones in a row, and then geared up for the fourth. He was just about to take off, Ollie panting happily at his side, when he spotted an odd sight near the church's side door.

Just about the whole town was standing around a pile of flowers, holding tiny white candles stuck in the bottom of paper cups. They were singing a depressing rendition of "In the Sweet By and By," but they stopped dead the moment they saw him, their faces gone white.

Miss Cleo even dropped her candle, and not a soul seemed to notice when her leopard-print loafer started sending up smoke.

"Sweet Jesus, protect us," called a frightened voice in the crowd.

CHAPTER FOUR
• AN UNWANTED VISITOR •

Miss Cleo kicked out her leg and hollered on account of the fire burning its way up her cream-laden toes. Her right loafer flew across the churchyard, landing not more than a foot from Gabe. Ollie promptly pounced, tearing at that shoe like it was a fuzzy squirrel dropped from heaven just for his benefit. Gabe would have laughed in any other circumstance, but the whole scene struck him as so dang strange his head started to throb.

"You didn't do all this for me, did you?" Gabe said, taking a step toward Miss Cleo. "All these flowers and candles and stuff? 'Cause I'm fine, just look at me. Better than fine, in fact."

Gabe waited for somebody to say something, but the only sound in the churchyard came from Ollie, as he disemboweled one-half of Miss Cleo's favorite pair of shoes.

"They'll never believe this down at the station," said Chip Evans, the voice of 107.3 Hip FM. He stared at Gabe like he was a bona fide apparition, and he kept fumbling for something in his pocket that turned out to be a camera. "No, sir, never in a million years."

"Somebody should call the cops, shouldn't they? Or the ambulance. No, no, better make it the cops," said Mr. Peters, talking to no one in particular.

Then Mrs. Higgins made her way through the crowd, her long black skirt billowing around her ankles. "Oh, how the wicked have risen from their graves," she said, in her best Sunday preacher voice.

That almost made Gabe wanna laugh, but somehow he didn't think she was joking.

"Shush, now," said Miss Cleo, but Gabe noticed she didn't come any closer or answer his question.

"Look, I understand how you might be confused," Gabe said reasonably, "seeing as I woke up in a funeral home. You all must've thought I was dead. But it's okay." Though it really wasn't. "Probably happens all the time, of course not so much since the Middle Ages, but I'm sure Doc Suthers did his best. Anyway, what's done is done, and I can assure you I've got no hard feelings." *Except maybe for that mangy chicken*, Gabe thought, but didn't say.

He took a step closer, and nearly everyone in the church-yard took a step back.

"I said I'm not angry, so don't go acting scared on my account!" Gabe said, growing more than a little ticked.

"And the sinners shall be punished," Mrs. Higgins intoned, her hair coming loose from its bun and swirling around her head like snakes. "The dead will walk and everyone left on this earth shall perish."

"That's not in the Bible," Miss Cleo said through tight lips.

"Neither is that." Mrs. Higgins held up a trembling hand, her bony finger pointing in Gabe's direction.

"Y'all can't be serious," Gabe said, his lighthearted tone starting to falter. "Come on, now, it's me. You made a mistake, that's all. Do I look dead?"

He threw out his arms, to prove his point, and every single eye zoomed straight to his belly. He peered down at the hole in his T-shirt, and his heart sank in his chest. There was something about that hole he hadn't noticed before, though he didn't quite see how he could have missed it. The edges weren't coated in mud at all. It was dark brown blood, and bits of it had splattered his jeans, too, and the rest of his T-shirt.

And just like that his neighbors started to run, some for the parking lot, others straight across the empty field behind the church.

"No mistake," said Mr. Lawson, standing his ground.

"But I'm right here, you can see me," Gabe said. Ollie sat down on Gabe's feet and started whining something awful at Gabe's feet. "I'm not going to hurt anyone."

There was a long silence. The few who had stayed started blowing out their candles and backing away.

"You'd better get on, now," Miss Cleo said after a while,

though she wouldn't meet Gabe's eyes. At least she hadn't run away. "You and your pup."

"Listen to your mama," said Mr. Lawson, folding his massive arms over his chest.

"She's not my mama," Gabe said. Anger bubbled up inside him, but it fizzled out at the look on Miss Cleo's face. Like he'd managed to slap her without even touching her. It was true, though. Miss Cleo wasn't his mama, and she'd never much tried to be. His real mama died when he was still a kid, on the same day as his daddy. Gabe wanted to live with Gramps once his parents passed, but then he'd up and died, too.

So, it'd fallen to Miss Cleo to take care of him, and even though she'd never been a mama to him, she hadn't turned him out on the street, either. And maybe that was something.

"Sorry, Miss Cleo." Gabe hung his head. "You believe me, don't you? I'm not some spook come back from the dead. Look." He pinched his skin to show that he was real.

Miss Cleo didn't answer. Danny Romero's parents patted Miss Cleo on the back and hurried to their car, and Gabe had never seen Ms. Sylvia Peabody, head of the Feral Cat Protection Committee, move so fast in her three-inch heels.

"Hold on, this must be some kind of joke. It must be!" Gabe closed the distance between him and Miss Cleo, meaning to talk some sense into her face-to-face, but Mr. Lawson blocked his path.

"No joke and no mistake." His jawbones worked back and

forth under his skin, like he was sharpening his teeth, getting ready to bite. Mr. Lawson wasn't the nicest fella in town, but Gabe had never known him to look quite so mean. "You'd better be on your way now, son."

That was when Pastor Higgins flew out of the church wielding the Christmas Eve candelabra like it was some kind of deadly weapon.

"Get away from my church, demon!" Pastor Higgins sliced the air with that silver candelabra, tripped over a rock, and fell flat on his face in the mud.

It was all so ridiculous that any other day Gabe would've laughed. Then he looked down again at the front of his T-shirt, and at the scared, sad expression on Miss Cleo's face. It might be ridiculous, but Mr. Lawson was right. This was no joke.

Now Gabe was the one backing away, the world going dizzy around him. He couldn't figure out how everything had gone so wrong so fast, and next thing he knew he tripped over a headstone and fell hard on the grass. The strange thing was, it didn't even hurt. He got up again, with Ollie's help, and took one last look at Miss Cleo.

"I guess I'll see you later, then," he said slowly, the full weight of his situation just beginning to dawn on him. Everyone in his life had already left him—his mom, his dad, Gramps—and now even Miss Cleo couldn't stand the sight of him. Not only that, the whole dang town seemed to think he was some kind of monster.

"I'm afraid this had better be goodbye. Not just for now," Mr. Lawson said. "For good."

Just then, a car screeched into the parking lot, and three boys scrambled out. Gabe's heart soared at the sight of them. It was Chance, Gabe's best friend, and his two older brothers. Surely Chance would believe him.

"There he is," yelled Jace, the oldest of the three. "Pa was right, he really is back. Let's get him."

Jace and Caleb, the middle brother, pounded over the crumbling parking lot toward them. Jace held an Easton Black Magic baseball bat. Gabe could tell, because it was the same one he'd left at Chance's house just last week. Caleb didn't have any kind of weapon, but that didn't matter much. He loved giving beatdowns, and Gabe knew from experience that his fists could hurt just as much as any bat. Chance stood by the car, mouth open, like he didn't know whether to join in or run.

"Chance!" Gabe called, but the look Chance gave him made every last bit of hope crumble to dust. There was disgust and fear and maybe a little bit of remorse in that look, but just a little. Chance didn't care what happened to him, not any more than Miss Cleo, that much was clear, and here Gabe was thinking best friends stood up for each other.

The brothers hit the grass without slowing down and every muscle in Gabe's body tensed. They weren't going to stop. It sounded too wild to be believed, but there it was. He looked over at Miss Cleo and Mr. Lawson, but neither raised their voice or made a move to stop what was about to happen.

Ollie tensed his forty-pound body and got ready to attack. That was when Gabe made his decision. He could take a beating, sure enough. After all, he'd done so on more than one occasion, but if anything happened to Ollie, he'd never forgive himself. Chance was alright, for the most part, but his brothers were what Miss Cleo called ill-bred. They'd spun a cat around by its tail once and flung it into a ditch. No way anything like that was going to happen to his dog.

"I guess this is it," said Gabe, to everyone and no one in particular. Miss Cleo had turned her back on him, her head buried in her hands, as if he were already gone. So much for a long, heartfelt goodbye. "Come on, boy, let's get out of here."

Gabe and Ollie took off running, jumping over gravestones like they were Olympic athletes. He didn't slow down, even when the grass turned to sharp rocks under his bare feet. Truth be told, they didn't hurt, not one little bit. Ollie, on the other hand, was panting something terrible, but he kept up as best he could. They'd just scaled the small iron fence surrounding the churchyard when something hard cracked into the back of Gabe's head.

He slowed down and fell forward, his face slamming into the grass. Ollie barked and snarled and snapped at the air.

"Don't touch him, man, let's get out of here," said a breathless voice somewhere behind him. "This is so *Evil Dead*, I'm serious, Jace, just leave him alone and let's go."

"No way," said Chance's eldest brother. "Do you want him coming back to eat your face off in your sleep?"

Gabe reached out, and his fingers found the thing that had hit him. It was a rock the size of a softball. He turned around, but not before another rock crashed into his cheek.

"Cut it out, man. Come on!" Caleb cried.

Gabe's ears were ringing and the whole world seemed to spin around him. Before he could figure out what to do, he saw a brown-and-black shape surge past him, aiming straight for the boys. He had to act fast. Ollie had teeth and jaws and good intentions, but he was no match for a rock the size of an asteroid.

Gabe bolted upright, just in time to see Jace get into a hitter's stance. Ollie was moving so fast, there was no way Gabe could stop him. Jace swung that bat, his eyes wide with fear, and something else, too. Like maybe he was enjoying this.

Ollie was hanging in midair now, his hair standing straight up like one long black sail.

"I told you to stop!" Caleb cried, but the words didn't reach Gabe's brain. He was too busy grabbing for his dog and screaming inside his head, since he knew he wouldn't make it. That bat kept right on coming, and Gabe stretched and stretched, preparing himself for the sickening crunch of breaking bones, but it never came.

What happened was this. Caleb pushed Jace hard in the chest just before the bat made contact, and he fell, hitting his left shoulder on a rock. Ollie skidded to the dirt, in the spot where Jace had been only a moment before. Spitting with rage, Jace sank his fist into Caleb's face, and a full-on brawl ensued.

Gabe didn't stop long enough to see who won, or even to say thank you. He picked Ollie up by the rump and ran as fast as he could, speeding away from the only place he'd ever lived and the only people he'd ever known.

CHAPTER FIVE
· THE LETTER ·

They kept on running till they found themselves deep in the woods. And then, Gabe only paused for a moment, to feel his head and cheek. To his surprise, he wasn't even bleeding. And the ache, if he felt any ache at all, was a small one. He cuddled Ollie a minute, to celebrate their narrow escape, and then they took off again, cutting a new path through the trees and the overgrown brush.

When Gabe was a kid, he'd always loved it when Gramps took him camping. They'd roast marshmallows and Gramps would tell him stories about rustling cows on the farm or flying bombers in World War II. Well, Gramps wasn't here.

Gabe was alone, more alone than he'd ever been, and camping alone wasn't all that fun.

As if in protest to his sullen thoughts, Ollie ran up and licked his ankle. "At least I got you, boy. I guess that means I'm never really alone."

Gabe picked up his step, trying to let that thought lift his spirits. It was true, Ollie was the best friend a boy could have.

What did it matter if he was a dog and not a person? People let you down. They turn their backs on you when all you ever tried to do was help.

Yup, he was better off just him and Ollie. "You're a true and loyal friend, you know that, boy?"

Ollie must have understood, because he gave Gabe one more fierce lick and then took off running. Gabe trotted after him, feeling a whole lot better about his predicament. Camping out still didn't prove to be much fun, though.

For one thing, Ollie picked up a tick about every one or two feet. Having a hungry tick bite into your bottom must not be that great, because Ollie kept gnawing at his rear end like he meant to chew it clean off. Gabe did the best he could to pull out the ticks without tearing off the heads, but that was easier said than done. By the time they'd made it a few miles, judging by the position of the sun, Ollie's bottom was itchier than a flea on a hot plate.

Gabe carried him a good part of the time, but Ollie was a sniffer dog, in spirit if not by credential, and he kept wiggling till Gabe had no choice but to set him free.

Once the sky turned from bright blue to soft purples and pinks, Gabe decided there was no way those boys were gonna follow them. Good, at least that was one less thing to worry about. He settled down beside a small creek, taking a seat in the shade. Ollie bounded into the water and drank for so long Gabe was surprised he didn't burst.

With his thirst satisfied, Ollie plopped down next to Gabe. He was panting hard, but Gabe was grateful to see he was still smiling. He leaned back, resting his head on a rock like it was a pillow. Maybe that would be his pillow for a while, at least until he could make Miss Cleo see sense.

Trudging through the woods all day had given him plenty of time to think, not only about his rotten luck but about where to go from here. The way he saw it, he only had one option. He had to sneak back into town next chance he got, despite those two mean brothers. If he could just explain things to Miss Cleo one-on-one, he was certain she'd understand. True, they'd never got along that great, and Miss Cleo could be mean when she wanted, but Ollie needed a home. A real home. Even if he did have to sleep out in the yard with the rotten eggs and chicken poop.

And maybe Gabe needed a home, too, even if he hated to admit it.

Yup, first thing next morning, Gabe would head back into town and make his case. That would give the brothers time to go back to what they were best at, skipping school and generally making other people's lives miserable. And Miss Cleo never left the house before eleven if she could help it, so as long as he made it back by then, he should be good. Miss Cleo wasn't the nicest or the most forgiving, but once he said his piece, he knew she'd see sense.

Gabe turned his attention to the sky, where the soft pinks

and purples slowly turned a peaceful shade of deep-ocean blue. He imagined fish flitting by, some small and shimmery, others so long the sky wasn't big enough to hold them. He took a deep breath, and to his surprise the air tasted fresh and cool and salty. The trickles of the creek turned into the reassuring roar of the ocean, at least in his mind.

It was just like Gramps had always said. "If you're feeling scared or worried or overwhelmed, picture something magical. Something big. Because then, all your fears will look small as gnats by comparison."

Gramps.

Was that what had happened that night in Miss Cleo's bed? He'd been scared and so he'd pictured something magical, his gramps come back from the dead? 'Cause he had died, just like his parents, nearly two years ago to the day. If only Death could have kept his nasty paws off him for once. Like it wasn't enough that he'd already snatched both of Gabe's parents. Then he could have convinced Gramps that he should live with him instead of Miss Cleo, and Miss Cleo would be nothing more than his mean old chicken-loving neighbor. No way Gramps would turn him out of his home, not even if he really did transform into some moldy, brain-eating zombie.

Oh well. Guess it should come as no surprise that Death, like life, wasn't always fair.

And what was it Gramps had said that night in his dream? He searched the back corners of his brain, trying to remember, but it was no use.

Apart from his final words, that is. He remembered those clear enough, because they were so strange. His very own gramps saying he was sorry.

"Sorry for what?" Gabe said, but Ollie didn't answer. He was fast asleep, tummy in the air, legs spread-eagled, snoring like a hog with a head cold.

Gabe must have drifted off, too, after a while, because the next time he woke up it was dark and chilly and something wet was wiggling inside the hole in his stomach.

He just about jumped out of his skin when he felt it, scrambling backward into an unfortunate collision with a tree trunk. He swiped at his tummy, like he was expecting to find a snake or a worm the size of a garden hose wiggling around where it shouldn't be. Instead, a familiar pointy nose nuzzled his chin, and then Ollie proceeded to kiss him rapid-fire on the lips.

Gabe managed to redirect his assault to his hands, but then, to his extreme discomfort, Ollie turned his attention once again to the hole.

"Quit it," Gabe pleaded, but when Ollie was on a mission, he was like a bee headed for honey.

He licked and smacked and slobbered, and the weird part was, Gabe didn't feel a thing. Apart from being ticklish, and wanting to throw up.

After a few minutes, Ollie finally started to grow tired, and Gabe felt around for a juicy-looking stick. With Ollie successfully distracted, Gabe sopped up the slobber on the inside of his T-shirt. He touched the hole on his stomach, gingerly, and then the one on his back. They lined up perfectly, as if he were one of those tiny party sausages, and someone had stuck him clean through with a toothpick.

He thought back to that wild evening, up on the roof with Princess Carmella. He remembered how she'd flapped just out of reach as he'd grabbed for her, and he remembered the sight of that twister coming down out of the sky like some giant, demonic finger. He even recalled how that twister had carried her off, the whine and the dusty, electrifying smell of it. Then he took hold of that weather vane, and his mind was blank after that.

A blank that ended with him sleeping rough in the woods with a rock for a pillow.

Gabe's pondering was interrupted by the steady pitter-patter of rain. As was often the case around these parts, it grew from a drizzle to a torrent in a matter of seconds. The thin tree branches provided little protection, and so they ran. Thankfully, Gabe had been out this way before, "getting up to no good," as Miss Cleo put it, so he knew there were some old caves on this side of Very, Very Tall Hill.

Very, Very Tall Hill, as its name implied, was the tallest hill not only in Macomb County, but in the whole dang world.

That was because it was just a few inches short of being considered the world's puniest mountain. Gabe and Ollie ran through the pounding rain and took refuge in the first cave they found.

It was dark and cold and it smelled like mildew growing over wet rock. As soon as they ducked inside, the rain stopped. Not stopped altogether, but it died down from a torrent to a polite purr.

Gabe shook his head, and even though it wasn't really that funny, he couldn't help but laugh. Not just about the rain, either. About the whole dang situation. Imagine him risking his life on account of a no-good chicken, trying to make Miss Cleo happy, and what thanks did he get for his troubles? None, that's what. At least, nothing apart from a big fat kick to the backside.

Ollie tensed and then shook off his fur right in Gabe's face. There was nothing to do but keep on laughing. That was always Gramps's philosophy, and it was his philosophy, too. Blissful and unaware of the shower his shaking had caused, Ollie turned around a dozen times before plopping down on the dirt and closing his eyes. Since they were both wet already, Gabe decided he might as well have somewhere better to rest his head than a rock, so he used Ollie as a pillow.

His body was extra warm, and his breathing soon soothed Gabe into a deep and restful sleep. When he woke up next, it was morning.

The sun was just peeking over the horizon when he emerged from the cave, so he knew he hadn't left it too late. He expected to feel exhausted, or at least a little tired, after his recent ordeal, but Gabe could have scaled a skyscraper if he'd gotten enough of a running start. At least, that was how his muscles felt. Like there were bands of energy coursing up and down his bones. As for his brain, it was a whole different story.

"Come on, boy, we've got a good jog ahead of us," he said, trying not to sound nervous. He knew it wasn't just the brothers he had to watch out for; it was Mr. Lawson and Pastor Higgins and the whole dang town, too. Not to mention what would happen if Miss Cleo chose not to listen, but Gabe refused to think about that, at least for the time being. "Don't worry, boy, we can do it!"

Ollie did not look quite so spry, even after his pep talk. Gabe estimated they had at least a five-mile journey back into town.

"Don't be scared, now. I won't let those dumb old brothers get you."

And that was a promise. After Ollie got a few gulps of water from the creek, they headed off. Gabe jogged nice and slow so Ollie could keep up, but after only a couple of minutes that dog plunked down in the grass and rolled over for a belly rub.

"Can't stop yet, you silly pup. Come on! Giddyup, now, it's a game!" Gabe sprinted off across an open clearing, sounding a lot cheerier than he felt. "See if you can catch me!"

Gabe ran as fast as he could to the nearest patch of trees. "Beat you!" Gabe said. He looked back and groaned about as deep and long as he'd ever groaned before. What was that dog doing, but waggling his legs in the air, waiting for a tummy rub?

That left Gabe with about one choice and zero other options. He jogged back across the clearing, hoisted Ollie over his shoulder, and took off running. Full disclosure: He gave him a belly rub first. Ollie might be stubborn and about as ornery as they come, but he was also a good dog.

As Gabe suspected, Ollie liked riding a lot more than he liked running. He spent the whole time sniffing and barking and wagging his tail. He was also in prime position to lick the back of Gabe's neck, and he was especially happy because there was nothing Gabe could do about it.

Gabe made it into town before the sun had fully risen in the sky. Not many people were out this early in the morning, so it wasn't hard to hide behind buildings and dumpsters and overgrown hedges on his way to Miss Cleo's house. That didn't mean his stomach wasn't churning something awful, though, at the thought of getting caught. He was glad to have Ollie squeezed tight to his chest. His warm doggie body made his nerves calm down, but only just a little.

Miss Cleo's house had lavender siding and an "I Love Jesus" sticker in every window. There was a hedge out front cut into the shape of a chicken and pinwheels of every size and color stuck here and there throughout the yard. Most of them were snapped and trampled now, on account of the storm.

A long walkway wound its way up to the front door, and at the start of that walkway was a small white mailbox decorated with miniature red hens and bright yellow daisies. Gabe had wanted one with green tractors on it, but Miss Cleo always had to get her way.

With a sigh, Gabe put Ollie down on the grass and stood there staring at the mailbox. The back of his throat started to tingle and feel heavy, like maybe he was about to throw up. He couldn't remember feeling this nervous since the day of Mama and Daddy's funeral. He'd stood outside that church for thirty whole minutes, too scared to go in, until Gramps had squeezed him tight, and he'd smelled his dusty, Bengay smell, and somehow his feet had started walking.

That day had been all about saying goodbye, even though his parents were already gone. Then he'd had to say goodbye to Gramps, too, not that long after. Gabe was fed up with saying goodbye. He hated that word. He hoped he never heard it again in his whole dang life.

Even from stubborn, mean, persnickety old Miss Cleo. Ollie needed a home and so did he, and when it came right down to it, Miss Cleo needed him, too. Who else would muck out the chicken coops or climb into the crawl space in search of dead animals stinking up the house? Nobody, that's who.

He just had to think of the right words to convince her. He closed his eyes, pondering, when a crinkling sound drew his attention. Ollie was nosing at a plastic bag tied to the mailbox.

Gabe bent down to investigate, and that was when he saw the note taped to the front of the box. It had his name written on it in Miss Cleo's shaky, curly script. He peeled it off and unfolded the thick purple paper.

Dear Gabe,

   You may not know it, but I care about you like you was my own son, and that's the truth. None of this is your fault, so don't you go thinking it is. I'll never forget what you did for my precious Princess Carmella. Those was the actions of a hero, sure enough.

The period trailed off at the end, and there was a smudge, like the paper had been wet and then dried again.

   Folks around here are saying what happened to you ain't natural. They're scared, and I'm sorry to say, so am I. Now, don't go getting upset, because I'm not angry at you. I'm really not. But the thing is . . .

The sentence ended there, but continued on the back of the page.

. . . you can't come home. It's not safe. Not for you, and not for me.

I've left some food to tide you over. Biscuits, too, your favorite.

I hope you can forgive me.

Goodbye now,

Miss Cleo

CHAPTER SIX
· THREE DAYS ·

Gabe was so stunned, he hardly even noticed when the letter fell from his fingers and got picked up by a gust of wind. It tumbled down the dusty gravel road, sticking on a thornbush, before tearing in two and getting trampled under the tires of a passing truck.

Good, Gabe thought, and he pictured that word getting trampled on, too. Smashed to nothing under the thundering wheels of the truck. Dang, stupid word. Goodbye.

He stood there, breathing hard for a while, and then Ollie started to whine. "Don't you worry, boy. Everything's gonna be okay." Though he sure as heck couldn't see how. Trying hard to catch his breath, he hiked up his pants and did the only thing he could. He kept on going. Even if he didn't want to. Even if his insides ached like they'd been washed and hung out to dry. Ollie needed him now more than ever, and he wasn't going to let his dog down.

"I guess that's that," Gabe said, gritting his back teeth. He wasn't about to get angry or cry or anything like that, even if

Ollie was the only one listening. Miss Cleo didn't care a lick about him, and so why should he care if she kicked him out of her stinky, chicken feather house?

Gabe stole one last glance at his former abode before leaving for good. A shadow crossed behind Miss Cleo's bedroom window. The curtains flickered, like maybe someone had been looking out, but then they settled back in place again and the shadow was gone. Gabe thought briefly about banging on her door and demanding to be let in, but he knew he wouldn't. It was one thing for Miss Cleo to say goodbye in a letter. Those cold words echoed in his head: You can't come home. It was another thing to hear it in person. He didn't think he could take it, and besides, Miss Cleo wasn't worth all this anger and heartache. No, sir, he'd heard the last goodbye he ever wanted to hear, and now it was time to move on.

He considered leaving the bag of food behind, out of pure hurt and spite, but Ollie would need to eat, and he sure didn't need to suffer on account of Gabe's pride. As for himself, if he was being honest, he didn't care if he never ate again.

Grabbing the plastic sack full of food and tying it around his belt, he took off down the road, Ollie sprinting to keep up. He didn't look back and he didn't shed a tear. Instead, he kept telling himself Miss Cleo wasn't worth it. He didn't need her, and neither did Ollie. They'd find a better home, a real home, where he didn't have to work all day just for a few scraps of food.

At the end of the road, Gabe bent down and pulled Ollie into a long, fuzzy hug. The dog leaned in, taking another opportunity to lick the back of Gabe's neck. When they were done hugging, Gabe figured he could keep on going, at least for a little while. Ollie wiggled his nose into the hole in the top of the plastic bag and came out holding one of Miss Cleo's charbroiled hot dogs. The sight made Gabe smile, and besides, that dog deserved a treat after everything that had happened.

After all, he was homeless now, and so was Gabe. Homeless. Without a home. He might've had some pretty rotten luck in his life, but this was by far the worst.

Gabe stood there, in the middle of Country Road 162, and he realized that for maybe the first time in his whole life, he had no clue what to do. Going home wasn't an option. His best friend, Chance, would sic his brothers on him sooner than take him in. Mr. Lawson had made it pretty clear he wasn't wanted around these parts, and he had no doubt the rest of his neighbors felt the same.

He paused, and it was like his feet were superglued to the ground, 'cause he couldn't seem to get moving. He kept looking back toward town, as if maybe he'd see Miss Cleo or Chance running after him.

'Course, real life didn't work that way, as Gabe knew darn well. If he crossed into that field and the woods beyond, there was no going back. Miss Cleo wouldn't follow him, she'd made that much plain, and he'd be well and truly on his own.

"Guess we got no choice," he said aloud, by way of convincing his feet to get moving. They didn't, though, and Ollie started to whine and chew on the bottom of his jeans. They were already frayed, from all the other times Ollie had set to chewing, and Gabe guessed they'd stay that way. Not like he was about to get another pair any time soon.

If only Miss Cleo would let him sneak in once a week to do the laundry. Surely that was a reasonable enough request. And food. One sack of food wouldn't last him very long out in the wild. Weren't there laws about abandoning children? "Sure, I should go to the police and turn Miss Cleo in," he said, knowing full well he wouldn't.

Besides, Sherriff Bantley had been at the church, hadn't he? If he'd wanted to do something about how Gabe was being treated, he'd have done it then.

"Awwooo!" Ollie howled, and Gabe knew just how he felt.

"We sure are in a serious predicament, boy, and no doubt about it." No sooner had the words left his mouth than Gabe had an idea. He could hardly believe the thought hadn't crossed his mind before. This whole thing had started when he'd woken up in the funeral home. That meant someone there must know what had really happened. They could prove to Miss Cleo that he wasn't really dead after all. Sure, it'd be risky, and it might not work, but what choice did he have? If there was a way to figure this whole dang thing out and get his home back, even if it was with mean old Miss Cleo, he had to try.

"Stick close, boy, and stay quiet."

Keeping to the bushes and back roads, Gabe made his way across town, Ollie on his heels. The closer he got to people and houses, the more his stomach twisted, until it was nothing but a big, tight knot. Relief washed over him as Morton & Sons Funeral Home finally came into view. Today, the sign by the road read, "If death is the next great adventure, why not travel in style? Try our new Majestic Dreams casket with adjustable headrest."

A cool breeze rattled the row of spindly trees in front of the cruel brick building. It looked that way to Gabe, cruel. All harsh angles and gray marble, so sharp you could cut yourself just by looking at it. The air was different here, too. Dusty and stinking faintly of chemicals, like all the life had been sucked clean out. Gathering up his courage, Gabe sidled around to the back door, the same one he'd stumbled out of just the day before. He turned the knob and was surprised to find it wasn't locked.

Inside smelled like Mr. Belcher's biology class the week they'd dissected a frog. Not that Gabe had so much as touched a scalpel. He'd tried his best to follow instructions, honest he had, but he'd ended up out in the hallway breathing into a paper bag. His partner, Emma Caldero, did double the work, and that day at lunch he got called a crybaby and a sissy and a whole bunch worse.

That cold, clammy feeling he'd had at the sight of that frog crept over his skin again, and his stomach gurgled like it wanted to turn inside out. The room was pitch-black, but he could smell the formaldehyde, and the idea that there might be a dead body hiding behind all that dark made his skin squirm.

"I thought you might be back," said a nasally voice from somewhere deep in the shadows.

Gabe jumped, he couldn't help it. Ollie clicked over the tiles and planted himself on Gabe's left foot. Gabe could tell he was scared, too, by the way his bottom didn't wiggle even the slightest bit.

"You must have a lot of questions. I know I would, if I found myself in your unfortunate situation. Not that I'm likely to ever do so, but still . . . unfortunate."

A bright light clicked on and there stood the thin, imposing figure of Mr. M. M. Morton. He wore a three-piece suit in a metallic shade of gray, with white gloves, white shoes, and a white polka-dot tie. *No, not dots*, Gabe thought, *skulls*. He looked, in a word, cruel. His papery skin lacked the slightest bit of color, like a wrinkled-up chicken breast fresh from the fridge.

"You're a first, my dear boy. I do hope you know how extraordinary that is. A true and utter original." Mr. Morton drew a gloved hand down the hollows of his cheeks, smoothing out his drooping, leathery skin. He had a smell about him that rose above the science-room stink. Like dead flowers mixed into a bowl of spoiled milk.

Gabe didn't say a thing, and he sure as heck didn't move an inch. Everything about Mr. Morton made him want to crawl up inside his own skin and never come out again. Even Ollie, who was braver than most dogs when it came right down to it, started to shiver and quake by his side. Suddenly, his need to get answers, to find a way to explain things to Miss Cleo, started to fade. Despite his dire situation, what he wanted to do now more than anything was run.

"But you look confused, poor lamb. Well, why wouldn't you be? It's not every day someone comes back from the dead." He savored those last few words, the way you do when you're trying to suck the final bit of sweetness from a piece of hard candy. Gabe's teeth sank into his bottom lip, but he didn't taste any blood. This definitely wasn't what he'd come back for.

"Oh dear, I've shocked you," continued Mr. Morton, twisting his face into a look of concern. "Do you mean to tell me you still don't know what happened?"

Gabe wanted to answer, but just then it was all he could do to keep from throwing up. He took a deep breath, trying to settle his stormy stomach. Maybe it was the stink or the way Mr. Morton's eyes seemed flat, like they were printed on copy paper and then glued back in place. Or maybe it was the empty metal table in the center of the room. It was empty now, praise be to heaven, but Gabe knew one fact for certain: It was the table Mr. Morton used to prepare the bodies.

"How about a nice cup of tea?" Mr. Morton was saying.

"With extra sugar. You don't look at all well, I hate to say. Come on, now, let's take a seat."

Mr. Morton reached for Gabe's hand, but he jerked it away. If Mr. Morton was offended, he didn't show it. He smiled, revealing two rows of stubby yellow teeth.

"I don't guess the dead would much enjoy a visit to a funeral home. Of course, most people don't." Mr. Morton set up two metal folding chairs and took a seat in the one farthest from the door. Gabe stared at his but didn't sit.

Mr. Morton waited in silence, tapping the tips of his fingers together and smiling, as if Gabe's ordeal were nothing more than a mild source of amusement.

"I'm not dead," Gabe managed, after his tummy settled down enough for him to speak. "I can't be, look at me. Miss Cleo and everyone, they've got it all wrong. You have to help me. Tell them it's all some big mistake."

"Mistake?" Mr. Morton's smile only widened. "I know about a dozen witnesses who'd claim different. They'd say you fell off a roof in the middle of a twister."

"I fell, sure, but I didn't die. You must know that. You can tell them what really happened. That they stuck me here when I wasn't even dead."

"I'm afraid those same dozen witnesses would swear you had the misfortune of a bad landing," continued Mr. Morton, ignoring Gabe's words.

"Bad how?" Gabe's heart should have been pounding away

in his chest, but it wasn't. His pulse should have been racing, but it was still as a roach in a microwave. He couldn't be dead, though, he just couldn't. 'Cause his stomach sure was churning. Twisting and churning, so that was something. Dead people didn't get stomachaches. Or maybe he was imagining it. Maybe he felt that way because that's how he imagined he was supposed to feel. No, no, it couldn't be. It couldn't.

Mr. Morton stood and opened one of the stainless steel drawers set in the wall. He took out a familiar piece of wrought iron.

"The weather vane?" Gabe said, his thoughts so scattered they might have been bits of debris caught up in that very same twister. Why was he bringing out that old thing? Why now?

"I can't say I care much for chickens myself, but it's got a sharp tip. Sharp and long." Mr. Morton drew his skinny finger up the rough metal point. "Given the right circumstances, I'd say it could skewer someone, wouldn't you? In one side and out the other." Mr. Morton made a little stabbing motion with the weather vane, and Gabe couldn't help but flinch.

His hand dropped to his stomach. No way what this old creep said could be true. How could he be dead if he was up and walking around? If he'd been stuck through with a weather vane, of all things, wouldn't he know it?

"It's all some huge dang mistake! A conspiracy. Don't you think I'd remember if all that had happened? Don't you think I'd know if I was dead?"

"Think back," Mr. Morton said. "Close your eyes and think back."

Gabe didn't like the idea of closing his eyes with Mr. Morton in the room, but he figured Ollie would defend him if he tried anything funny. Besides, he had to know. That's what he'd come here for, wasn't it? The truth. He closed his eyes, and just like that he was back on the roof watching Princess Carmella drift up into that angry gray sky. Gabe's fingers wrapped around that weather vane, holding on tight as all heck, and then that demon finger reached down out of the sky and came for him. It lifted him into the air, that much he remembered, and then he fell. Like a roller coaster ride, but without any of the thrill.

All that was clear as day. The falling part, at least. But Mr. Morton was right about one thing, there must be something else. He closed his eyes even harder, glimpsing the swirling clouds, feeling the whipping wind. And then, there it was, an image he'd only just now remembered. The weather vane flying from his fingers, and him and that nasty old piece of iron free-falling side by side.

Then he hit the ground with a crack, and that was it. Only maybe it wasn't. Maybe he did remember something pinching into his back, right at that very last second before he passed out, and maybe he had seen it slice right through him like a toothpick through Jell-O, only he hadn't wanted to remember. If he squeezed his eyes even tighter and breathed deep, he could almost feel the tip of that weather vane, cold and rough and wet, protruding from the front of his shirt.

Gabe opened his eyes.

He didn't speak for a while, his lips numb. It was all he could do to keep from throwing up. Ollie grew restless and started chewing on his shoelaces.

"But I'm not dead," Gabe repeated, swallowing hard. "I'm here. So even if it happened like you said, even so, there's no way I can be dead."

Mr. Morton considered for a moment, and then he asked a question Gabe wasn't expecting. "Do you know what day it is?"

"What does that matter?"

"Do you? I'd be curious to know."

"Sure I do. Why wouldn't I? It's Thursday."

Just then, the church bell started to toll. Not the regular chime that marked every hour, but the full-length song that called people to worship.

"Sunday?" Gabe said, feeling like a weight was slowly pressing down on his shoulders. "Can't be."

"Three days," Mr. Morton said. "That's how long you laid on this table after you were dead. Three days for me to get you ready, so to speak. Do you know what we do here, to get a body ready for burial?" Mr. Morton tried on a sad face, but his eyes were still smiling.

Gabe didn't answer. He'd seen enough TV and read enough books to know what Mr. Morton meant. His stomach seized, like he was gonna lose his lunch right then and there, and then something inside him snapped. Like popping a rubber band in a big, empty chamber. And he was empty, wasn't he? A cold piece of meat with all the warm bits drained out. He clapped his hands over his mouth, but he didn't throw up. How could he? Throwing up was something normal people did, when they were still alive, and he was . . .

Dead. He was really dead. Like Mama and Daddy and Gramps. Dead as a dormouse in a snowstorm, that's what Miss Cleo would have said.

The facts seemed undeniable, but Gabe was still shaking his head. He couldn't accept it, he just couldn't. A headache bloomed behind his left eye, pounding and throbbing and getting bigger by the second. It was this place. This cruel, cold, horrible place. Why'd he ever think he could come here for help?

He'd had enough. He snatched up Ollie, holding his warm body tight to his meat locker of a rib cage.

"We shoulda never come here, Mr. Morton, and so this is goodbye." For once, he relished the word.

"Sorry to say, but not a soul around here will take you in," Mr. Morton said, though he definitely wasn't sorry. "We could make a deal, though, you and I."

Mr. Morton slid in front of Gabe, quick as a viper, placing one veiny white hand on the door. "Nobody will believe it till they see you. But, oh, when they do." He laughed. It was a raspy, metallic sort of laughter. "Well, let's just say, I'm sure we could come to some sort of arrangement. You need a friend, after all."

Gabe pulled on the knob, but Mr. Morton slammed the door shut.

"Look at yourself," he said. "Where will you go? What will you do, without me, that is? How long do you think that mutt'll survive without food?"

That made Gabe pause. Part of him was furious that Mr. Morton dared bring up his dog. It may not have been a threat, but it was close enough. The other part of him, though, knew Mr. Morton was right. One bag of food from Miss Cleo wouldn't be enough to feed Ollie forever, maybe not even for a week. If Mr. Morton had a way to make money, maybe he should hear him out. Even if he was as rotten as a slimy old piece of meat. For Ollie's sake.

"That's my boy," Mr. Morton said, snaking an arm around Gabe's shoulders and leading him away from the door. Ollie started to growl low and deep in the back of his throat the minute Mr. Morton touched him. Gabe sure didn't blame him, but maybe Mr. Morton knew a thing or two. A dog needed food and a bed and a place to call home.

Gabe turned, and saw his reflection in a small, square mirror screwed to the wall. He gasped.

He'd seen a corpse before, sure enough, at Mama and Daddy's and Gramps's funerals. He remembered Gramps the clearest. He'd looked just like himself, like he was sleeping, only at the same time he hadn't. Gabe could never put his finger on exactly why, but there was no way he could have mistaken Gramps for anything but dead. That was how he looked. Not bad, not horrible or moldy or peeling, but dead. Definitely dead. Somehow knowing it and seeing it were two entirely different things. Gabe started to shake from somewhere deep down, even with Ollie's hot body pressed against his chest.

"I can help you," Mr. Morton was saying, closing his other slithery hand around Gabe's wrist. "We'll be famous. More than famous, we'll be rich. You and I. We can do anything we want, go anywhere we please. Everyone in the whole world will want to know your name."

"And Ollie?" Gabe said.

Mr. Morton couldn't stop a look of disgust from creeping onto his face at the mere mention of his dog. That made up Gabe's mind right then and there. That, and the fact that Ollie was now barking at the top of his lungs and struggling to be freed.

Gabe tried to wrench his hand out of Mr. Morton's grasp, but the old man only held tighter.

"You can't survive without me, don't you understand? We'll make millions. Millions of millions. People will pay anything to touch you, to talk to you, just to look at you."

"Let me go!" Gabe cried, and he stamped down as hard as he could on Mr. Morton's foot.

The old man grunted and released his grip, but he was fast, too. Gabe had only opened the door an inch when Mr. Morton grabbed him by the shoulders and yanked him backward. All might have been lost if Ollie hadn't leapt and sunk his jaws into Mr. Morton's arm. Gabe heard a crack, and then Mr. Morton let loose a full-throated shriek.

"That-a-boy," Gabe said, and together they shot out the door and ran as fast as their feet would take them.

CHAPTER SEVEN

• VOICES IN THE WOODS •

They nearly got flattened by a car at the corner of Flint and Unnamed Road. It was a pink station wagon with "Honk if you love Jesus" painted down the side in glittery letters. The driver slammed on the brakes, and then promptly backed up directly into a phone pole. Gabe would have stopped and helped, despite his present predicament, but the driver pounded on the gas and shot on down the road, blasting Gabe with a wave of dust and smoke. That car had a crushed bumper and at least two flat tires, but fear made people do funny things.

He'd know that old station wagon anywhere, of course. It belonged to Mrs. Higgins, the pastor's wife. And she wasn't afraid of a baseball bat or some creepy mortician; she was afraid of him. Just like everybody else, except for nasty old Mr. Morton.

Full of anger and spite and still crackling with fear, he picked Ollie up again and his run turned into a sprint.

Sprinting turned out to be easy now that he was dead, despite the plastic bag banging into his thighs. Soon, he'd left the town far behind and was running through a big stretch of empty field. There were no sounds to bother him, apart from the tall grass crunching under his feet and the wind whipping his cheeks.

That was good, because Gabe needed some silence to help him think. There were so many thoughts spitting and fighting in his head, it was hard to wrap his mind around just one. He'd only felt like that a few times before. The day of Mama and Daddy's funeral, for one. Like his mind was full of wasps and he'd never be able to see straight or think straight again. And it was true. Everything had changed after that, so much so that he hardly remembered how things had been before. Before them dying and him going to live with Miss Cleo. He hadn't wanted to forget about them, but he had. Like how they smelled and exactly what Mama used to look like when she smiled.

A branch slapped Gabe across the cheek, and he slowed down, but only a little. Ollie started to squirm and grow restless in his arms.

"Sorry, boy. Not much farther." He didn't want to, but he started to cry, screwing up his face and gasping for air. His cheeks ached something awful, but no matter how hard he tried to get it all out, not a single tear came loose. "Guess I can't even cry right," Gabe said.

Ollie licked his chin, and he kept on going. The woods grew thicker as he went, closing in around him. Soon, the tall grass was gone, replaced with cool black mud. All the sounds of the town disappeared, too, even the buzzing from the electrical power plant. Gabe pulled to a stop for a moment, listening to the leaves and the quiet roar of crickets.

"Just you and me," he said, peering around at the dark tree trunks and the long gray trails of Spanish moss. "Don't worry, boy, we'll be alright."

About an hour or two later, they came to a creek cutting a jagged path through the trees. Ollie took a big, long gulp and then went to work splashing in the water. Gabe knelt down, too, and scooped some chilly liquid into his palms. He realized he hadn't taken a drink himself this whole dang time. He brought the water to his lips and swirled some around inside his mouth. He tried to swallow, but it was like someone had shut a door in his throat and thrown away the key.

No matter what he did, the water kept dribbling out again. Ollie bounded over, soaking wet and pawing at the plastic bag. He wiggled his bottom and whined something awful. He was such a pathetic sight, Gabe couldn't help but laugh. The sound felt weird after all that crying, like it didn't belong to him, at least not anymore.

He removed the bag from his belt and looked inside. There were three apples from the tree behind Miss Cleo's house. He'd always called it that, Miss Cleo's house, instead of his house or their house or home. Now it was really true. Maybe that was what Miss Cleo had wanted all along. Gabe allowed himself one long sigh before continuing.

He lined up the shiny red apples on the grass. Ollie touched each one with his nose, and then snarfled in Gabe's general direction. A snarfle was kind of like a bark and a snort combined, but Ollie only did it when he really wanted something bad, or when he was just plain excited.

"Okay, you stubborn mutt. Let's see what else we got."

He fished around in the bag and came out with a whole ziplock bag full of charbroiled hot dogs, a Tupperware container packed with homemade tuna salad, and a dozen of Miss Cleo's sweet-and-savory biscuits wrapped in foil. Those were Gabe's favorite, or at least they had been. They were kind of like regular biscuits, except they were filled with chunks of salty bacon and swirls of sugary syrup.

Ollie snarfled again, so Gabe tossed him a hot dog. He gobbled it up in all of three seconds, and then started nudging Gabe's hand, asking for more. Gabe figured he'd better wait a few minutes before giving him another, otherwise he'd only throw it all up again.

"Hush, now, and stop being so dramatic."

As could be expected, his words had little effect, so he did his best to ignore Ollie and turned his attention to the biscuits. As soon as he unwrapped the foil, he was aching to take a bite, despite his anger at Miss Cleo. It must have been his imagination, but it seemed like the biscuits in the middle were still warm. He removed one of the warm ones and held it against his lips. The smell was happy and sad, all at the same time. He loved Miss Cleo's biscuits something fierce, so that was happy. The sad part was that he knew now how little Miss Cleo cared for him. These biscuits weren't filled with love, just butter and sugar and a whole lot of bacon.

Even so, a still-warm biscuit was too much for his tummy to resist. He sank his teeth into the crispy outer shell. He wasn't disappointed. The rich taste of bacon tingled on his tongue, mingling with the sweet, sticky syrup.

He swallowed down that first bite, ready for the second, when a strange thing happened. Just like the water had dribbled out the edges of his mouth, the food didn't want to go down. He tried again, taking a big gulp, but that food kept coming back up.

Finally, he had no choice but to spit it on the ground and wash his mouth out with water. Staring at those slobbery chunks was one of the worst moments of his whole entire life. Without warning, his face crumpled up and he started to dry heave.

"Just quit it!" he said, a hot wave of shame and confusion sweeping over him. He'd never cried so much in his whole dang life, and he couldn't even conjure up any tears. He wasn't a crybaby, he really wasn't!

Ollie bounded over and started licking his face, which made him feel the tiniest bit better. At least someone still cared about him. Ollie curled up in his lap, and slowly Gabe's breathing returned to normal. "Don't you fret, now, you hear?" Gabe said to Ollie, scratching his chin. "We'll be fine, you and I." Saying the words out loud, Gabe just about believed them. Even if they might freeze to death or starve in the woods all alone. Even if Gabe felt more lost than he ever had, apart from the day Gramps came over to tell him Mama had died.

Now he was the one who was dead, and he had a pack of eleven and a half uneaten biscuits to prove it. Gabe sat there by the stream for a long while, his head buried in Ollie's fur. He didn't see how things would end up alright, but he had to pretend. For Ollie's sake.

Pushing away the late-afternoon shadows that seemed to coil around him like snakes, he tied up the bag and decided they should go a bit farther on. No use sticking close to town, since he was about as welcome there as an ant on a wedding cake. He tried not to let that thought depress him as he pushed even deeper into the forest. He didn't know all that much about the area, except that the trees went on for miles and miles, all the way to the state line.

They walked till going on nightfall, Ollie stopping every few feet to sniff or pee or sniff some more. Every now and then, he trotted back to check on Gabe, nosing his shins and slobbering on his bare toes. Gabe was still full of that strange energy, but he couldn't bring himself to do much else but slump forward, dragging one foot after the other, offering Ollie an occasional, everything's-going-to-be-okay smile.

Later, when the sun had dipped just below the horizon, Ollie darted off ahead, yipping and hopping with alarm.

"What is it?" Gabe said, ready for just about anything. He didn't think anyone could find them all the way out here, but he couldn't be sure.

"Rarf!" Ollie said.

Gabe ran to catch up and his heart settled back down in his chest. It was a campsite, complete with a metal grill, a tent pad, and a stack of leftover firewood. "Ain't that something? You really are a sniffer dog."

Gabe rewarded Ollie with a chunk of bacony biscuit. His heart broke a little to see him swallow it down whole, without even really tasting it. Oh well. He couldn't expect a dog to understand the subtleties of fine cooking.

"Might as well settle in here for the night." Gabe went about starting a fire, and Ollie helped by gathering bits of stray wood.

By the time the sun disappeared behind the trees, the fire was snapping and crackling. Gabe watched the dancing flames, remembering those chilly nights when Gramps would tell him spooky stories around the campfire. His stories always started out scary but turned funny by the end. With the monster exploding or turning into something harmless, like a stuffed animal.

He missed Gramps, the way he missed Mama and Daddy. All the people Death had taken from him. Gramps had always been such a good listener, giving him advice and arguing with Miss Cleo on his behalf. Now he was one of those missing souls, taken away from his home by that no-good Grim Reaper.

Partly out of frustration, and partly as a test, Gabe stuck his finger right in the middle of one of those dancing flames. It tickled his skin and singed his fingernail, but it didn't hurt a lick, the same way his bare feet didn't hurt after all that running.

With a big old sigh, Gabe turned away from the fire and fashioned Ollie a bed out of a mound of soft dirt. As soon as Ollie settled in, Gabe flopped down and used him as a pillow. He really was the best pillow ever, since he was warm and squishy and just the right size. Lying there like that, with Ollie's breathing to calm him down, he felt the tiniest sliver of hope for the future. He was out in the world all alone, sure, but he wasn't lonely. Not as long as he had Ollie by his side.

Together, they peered up at the stars, except Ollie might really have been sleeping. Gabe watched the full moon drift slowly from east to west. He pushed away all thoughts of Miss Cleo and Chance and Mr. M. M. Morton. Instead, he tried to remember what Gramps had said the day he'd come to visit. It seemed nearly impossible, but by then, Gabe must have already been dead.

Gramps had reached out his hand, like he was going to take Gabe somewhere. To heaven, maybe, or into the bright light. Wasn't that what was supposed to happen when you died? Then why had Gramps pulled back at the last second? Why had his old, wrinkled eyes looked so sad?

Maybe it had something to do with him saying he was sorry. Gabe remembered that part the most, but not the details of it. Why had Gramps felt the need to apologize? What on earth did he have to be sorry for?

And, more important, why had Gramps left without taking Gabe along with him?

All these questions were bouncing around inside his head, and so he didn't hear the voices at first, calling from off in the distance.

Ollie heard them, though, and he froze, every hair on his back going rigid under Gabe's skin. Gabe sat up, waiting. He figured it must be some kind of animal, a bear or a bobcat, but then he heard it.

Twigs snapping somewhere not too far away. And a voice, no, more than one. Voices that were calling his name.

CHAPTER EIGHT
· BULLETS IN THE DARK ·

Gabe did his best to stamp out the flames so no one could find them, but they roared all the way up past his knees. No sooner had he started than the leg of his pants caught fire, and he had to roll around in Ollie's dirt bed to put it out again.

"Where are you, zombie brains?" called a voice that turned his blood to ice. It was Jace, and Gabe heard other sets of footsteps, too, trailing not far behind. He flashed back to that day in the churchyard and the mean, wild look in Jace's eyes. He would've hurt Ollie bad if Caleb hadn't stepped in. Now he'd come back for more.

Gabe tried to figure out a plan, but everything was happening too fast. To make matters worse, with the dark and the trees and the way sounds tend to echo in the woods, Gabe couldn't tell which direction the voices were coming from.

"We're gonna have to run," Gabe whispered in Ollie's ear, his tongue dry as a prune in a tanning booth. "You stick close to me, you hear. Close as close can be."

"Hey, freak-o, I know you're out here. Didn't anyone ever teach you to cover up your tracks?"

Gabe forced his body to stay still, despite his insides, which were shaking something awful. With no other sounds to distract him, he searched the darkness, trying to figure out where Jace could be. If Jace had almost clobbered Ollie once, what would he do now that he was twice as mad?

"Over there!"

Gabe spun around, expecting to see Jace or Caleb wielding his old baseball bat, but there was no one. At least not that he could tell. The dark was so thick he could barely see a foot in front of him, and the flames of the still-burning fire made it worse, casting an orangey glare on the space between the trees.

"Gotcha, dead boy." To Gabe's horror, the footsteps crashing through the brush sped up. No doubt they'd spotted the fire and were running this way. Where were they? Were they closing in on him? Which direction should he run?

"Say, my buddies and I have a question for you, freak!" Jace's voice echoed off the trees. He was breathing heavier now, shouting and sprinting at the same time, that same snarl lighting up his words. "We wanna know if zombies still bleed!"

Gabe couldn't wait any longer. He still didn't know where they were coming from, but he had to choose a direction, any direction. He broke into a run. "Come on, boy, follow me!" Ollie growled and whimpered and then growled some more.

Gabe could tell he wanted to attack the voices, but it was too dangerous. "Now, boy! This way!"

Ollie ran, but he kept right on grumbling. He couldn't help it. It was in his nature to know when Gabe was scared and to try his best to defend him. Trees darted past on either side as Gabe coaxed Ollie on. They were going so fast, Gabe only had a few seconds to swerve around one tree before another popped up right in his path. He couldn't see the ground, so he had to trust he wasn't stepping into a trap or a hole that he'd never see the bottom of.

"You still there, boy?" Gabe said, and then he wished he hadn't.

Ollie barked, and that was when the whole world crashed in around them. A shadow heavy as a wrecking ball knocked Gabe to the ground and started pounding away at him with fists like steel. Gabe's jaw cracked and a second later he all but swallowed a tooth. A boot sank into his side next, over and over, and then there was someone yelling.

At first, he thought it might be Caleb, yelling at them to stop, but not this time. It was Ethylene Roberts, laughing at the top of her lungs, a frantic, frightened sort of laughter.

If Gabe had still been Gabe, he probably would have died all over again, right then and there. As luck would have it, he wasn't the same boy who'd once gotten his head stuffed down the hole of Mr. Benton's outhouse. The blows shook him up, sure enough, but they didn't hurt. No, sir. Gabe was different now. Those hateful, no-good brothers were right. He was a zombie freak-o dead boy, and he was sick of letting life, and Chance's brothers, beat him down.

It took all his might, but he wriggled free of the knee Jace had planted in his chest. He scrambled to his feet, and for the first time in his whole entire existence, he pulled back his fist.

He couldn't see any better than before, but he was getting ready to strike all the same, when he heard a sound that turned his blood cold.

There was a hard, dull whack, like someone swinging a bat at a punching bag, followed by a yelp. It was Ollie, no doubt about it.

Every muscle and tendon and nerve in Gabe's body stood at high alert. Somehow, he heard that bat swish through the air again, and he knew it was heading straight toward his dog. Without thinking or aiming or praying, he reached his hand into the darkness and grabbed that dang bat right out of mid-air. He shouldn't have been able to stop it, but he did. He wrenched it free and Ethylene's shrill laughter went dead quiet.

The clouds must have parted overhead just then, letting in a sliver of moonlight, because Gabe caught a glimpse of Jace's and Caleb's nasty, rotten faces. He expected their eyes to be blazing and savage, like the wild beasts they were, but more than anything they looked scared. Two skinny, scared boys with a brute of a daddy and a lot more guts than brains. Gabe couldn't see Ollie, not right then, and that was probably a good thing.

If he had seen him, he might not have said what he did.

"Go on, get the hell out of here. I mean it."

Ethylene didn't wait. She took one look at his face, and the bat he was holding, and she ran. Jace and Caleb stood their ground for a minute, but then Gabe jerked his body in their direction, and they took off like a pair of rats at a firing range.

"If I see you again, you're dead!" Gabe shouted at their backs. "Deader than dead. And it won't be like me, 'cause I'll make sure you never come back!" Gabe was shaking when he said it, but in that moment he meant every word. Not only that, but he knew how the brothers thought. Being honest and neighborly wasn't in their nature. But threats, well, that was one part of life the brothers understood.

Gabe was still shaking when the moonlight shifted a little, and he saw Ollie lying on his side, just like he was sleeping. His left back foot was bent at the wrong angle, and his fur was slick with blood.

Gabe sank to his knees to try and wake him, his chest swelling with fear at what he saw. He held his fingers close to Ollie's nose, and thanked God in heaven when he found that it was still wet. What was more, a warm, shuddery breath tickled Gabe's fingertips.

"Praise the Lord and all his angels. Why'd you have to try and help me fight? Why couldn't you have run?"

Now Gabe really was crying, tears and all, but he hardly even noticed. He was considering the best way to lift Ollie up when a light appeared not twenty feet away, glowing orange among the trees. Another light appeared, and then another and another. The next thing Gabe knew, a shot rang out.

"He's over there!" a voice called, and he knew without a doubt it was Jace.

To his horror, an entire army of feet trampled the brush, making its way toward him. More lights burned in the distance, four, five, and then at least a dozen.

"Don't let him get away!" A shiver of fear jolted down Gabe's spine, because that wasn't Jace or even Caleb, it was Mr. Lawson.

Another shot cracked in the darkness. They were only ten feet away now. Gabe fumbled with Ollie, no time to worry about his shattered leg. He pulled him close to his chest and did the only thing he could. Despite every muscle screaming in protest, despite the fear scorching into his gut, the certainty that a bullet would bury itself in his body at any moment, he ran.

He looked back once as he was sprinting through the thick brush. That was a mistake, because in that one awful moment he saw their faces. Mr. Lawson and Pastor Higgins. Elmer from the Pump 'n' Save and Mrs. Romero, her skirt hiked up past her knees. They were all racing toward him, flashlights casting cold orange shadows down their faces. Faces that looked more like masks than people. Masks etched with a hatred so pure and alive it was like a whole separate person, like a beast ready to tear him apart piece by piece. These had been his friends, his neighbors. The people who had promised to look out for him, after Mama and Daddy had died.

"Shoot, Jimmy. I see his face. Shoot!"

The rifle blasted again. There was no time to move, to think, to jump out of the way. It wasn't like the movies, when time froze and he could see the bullet coming. Instead, a weight struck him from the side and he hit the ground hard, Ollie tumbling from his arms.

If it was possible to die twice, he was pretty sure he'd just done it. He felt around desperately for Ollie, and for the hole where the bullet had hit him, but didn't find either.

"Get up, quick, and be quiet about it," an unfamiliar voice whispered in his ear. "And you'd better take your dog."

She, for the voice belonged to a girl, placed Ollie gently in Gabe's arms. He didn't have time to be grateful, but he was all the same. It came in the form of a cool ripple that rushed through his body, beating back the fire of everybody's hate.

"Hurry up, now," she said, and she was right.

Mr. Lawson and Elmer and the others were closing in on them. Just a few feet away.

"He's moving!" Elmer called.

Gabe heard Mr. Lawson cock back the rifle.

"Trust me," the girl said, and she grabbed Gabe's sleeve and pulled him into a thicket of bushes just as another bullet bit into a tree trunk an inch from his head.

CHAPTER NINE
• INTO THE MIST •

They twisted left and right, those pounding boots and orange lights never far behind. The clouds must have scooted back in place overhead, because the moonlight dried up and they ran in complete darkness.

"Do as I say, you hear?" said the girl, tightening her grip on his sleeve. She was running so fast, he could barely keep up and carry Ollie at the same time. Her voice sounded strange, though he couldn't think why.

"Don't worry, not much farther now."

She pulled him into what felt like the center of a tree. Twigs and thorns scraped against his skin. In his arms, Ollie woke up and started to moan.

"Shhh, buddy, gotta be quiet," Gabe said.

Behind them, the voices grew louder. They were far enough away now that he couldn't make out what they were saying, but they were coming, they'd heard him, he was sure of it.

"It'll be alright, I promise," the girl said. "Keep going."

She led him through thick brambles that grabbed at his ankles and wild vines that whipped against his face and arms. He was certain she must have made a wrong turn until he saw a faint, silvery light shining up ahead.

"What's that?" he said as they emerged into a clearing. The air felt different here, cooler and lighter, but at the same time heavy with mist.

"That is Bone Hollow," said the girl, squeezing his elbow with her small, cold hand. "You'll be safe there."

He peered into the mist that streamed across the valley in waves. Like a school of fish flitting to and fro, reflecting back the light.

"But they'll find us," Gabe said, his awe wearing away under the weight of all that panic. "Come on, we have to turn out the light."

He squeezed Ollie tighter and ran off into the mist, searching for the source of the light, but the girl didn't follow. She laughed. It was quiet and musical, and Gabe thought he'd never heard anything like it.

"Didn't I say not to worry?"

"But they have a gun," Gabe called over his shoulder, not slowing down one tiny bit. "They want to kill us. Me, at least, and maybe you, too!"

"I know," the girl said, speaking to him from the shadows, calm as a cucumber. He stopped just then and turned back to examine her. She was nothing more than a shadow wrapped in mist; he still hadn't seen her face. "But they won't find us. Not even if they search all night."

"How can you know for sure?" Gabe didn't understand it, but already he'd started to calm down. Like maybe she was right, and there was something about this place that meant they wouldn't be able to find it. What had she called it? Bone Hollow?

"I just know," said the girl, and then she stepped into the light. For a strange moment he thought he recognized her. The way her deep brown hair reached down past her waist, with one strand woven through with gold thread. Her eyes, one brown, one hazel. Her fairyland nose and chin, and her skin that had always reminded him of fresh-turned earth bathed in sunlight. Surely this must be Niko, his very first best friend, but it couldn't be. She'd moved away to California after third grade.

"You're smiling," she said, amused.

Gabe looked down, as if trying to glimpse the smile still on his face, but then Ollie moaned again and the spell was broken.

Panic sprouted in Gabe's throat at the sight of Ollie's bloody back paw. He had to do something, to get out of here, or turn off that dang light, or something.

"You're both safe and sound, I swear," said the girl, her voice full of comfort and reassurance.

Gabe had to admit he did relax a little at her words, despite himself. It had been lucky, hadn't it, her finding him out here in the middle of the night. Maybe too lucky. And what about that name? Bone Hollow? The very idea made him shiver.

"We'd better go inside," said the girl who might be Niko, just as Gabe heard the faraway call of voices coming from beyond the hedges.

He was certain they would break in. His muscles pinged and stretched, and his fingers dug into Ollie's fur, getting ready for whatever was to come.

"Follow me," said the girl, without a worry in the world. She swept past him in her lacy white dress, heading toward the light.

Gabe hesitated. Not because he was scared, not exactly. Surely the real danger was behind him, trying to find a way in. It was just something about how that dress clung to the girl's body when she moved. Like there was nothing underneath, no skin or muscles, just bone.

And her face. As if she could read his thoughts, she turned around at that exact moment and winked. For some reason that wink made him shudder even more. Surely, it was Niko, only she was older now, his age. But her skin and eyes. They looked different. He thought of the image he'd seen of his own face in the mirror at the funeral home, and then he took a step back toward the hedges.

"Not that way," said the girl, and there was a sudden urgency to her voice, like maybe she wasn't just being helpful, like maybe she needed him to stay.

Then Ollie started whining and moaning in his arms, and it was all Gabe could do not to break down crying at the sound of it.

"You're gonna die, freak!" Those words drifted through the thicket, like a message carried across a vast ocean. They sounded far away and close all at the same time. Anger pooled in the back of Gabe's throat, and Ollie wriggled and cried out in pain.

"Just a little bit farther," said the girl. She'd come back, and now she was standing just a few feet away, reaching out her hand.

Part of him knew, true or not, that if he took her hand there was no going back. He knew it the same way he'd known that once he'd kissed Maisy Hughes on the mouth his life would never be the same. Mostly, that was because her daddy had knocked out two of his teeth, but still, he'd felt different inside after that, too.

He looked down at her hand, and for a moment he didn't see Niko's hand at all, warm and inviting and familiar. He saw long thin bones, scraped clean and polished white. Behind him the voices bellowed, in his arms Ollie cried out in pain. All around, the waves of that glittering ocean seemed to buzz in his ears. Were they pulling him forward, or dragging him down underneath the water? If only Gramps were here, if only he could help.

"Listen to the ocean," whispered a voice in his ear.

Gabe spun around, but of course no one was there. Gramps

had always told him that, though. "Listen to the ocean." Even though Macomb County was about as landlocked as you could get, Gabe knew what he meant. The ocean was like his dreams and the sky and all the possibilities in the world smashed up into one.

"Listen," Gramps said.

The girl inched her hand closer. It wasn't bony anymore, but soft and brown. Gabe didn't know what to think or who to trust anymore, but he knew Ollie needed help bad. He might even die if he didn't move fast, and that was more than enough reason for Gabe.

He took the girl's hand, and together they walked into Bone Hollow. The odd thing, the truly unusual thing, was that the closer they got to that eerie white light, the more distant the voices sounded. Like they were drifting away across that peaceful ocean, leaving their angry, hate-filled yells back on the shore.

They descended into a small valley, where all the mist had collected, just like someone had scooped it off the top of a pot of boiling stew. Except this mist was cool and it smelled like wood and fresh-cut grass. Ollie was still moaning something awful, but once in a while as they walked he stopped to take a bite of the mist, and that made Gabe's heart sing. Lit from behind the way it was, those tiny water droplets looked for all the world like miniature stars. Ollie gobbled them down with a weak snarfle, and then went right back to crying.

"It's just over here," said the girl, and they emerged from the mist to the sound of tinkling music. Gabe couldn't tell where it came from at first, but then he saw dozens of hand-carved flutes dancing in the breeze. They were dangling from the roof of a small cottage, overgrown with ivy and mint and vines Gabe had never seen before, and, shimmering in the flower beds encircling the cottage, glittering blue buds.

"They bloom brightest at night," the girl said, but Gabe was more interested in the flutes. They clinked together, making a pleasant but peculiar sort of music. It reminded him of a wind chime Elmer had put out in front of the Pump 'n' Save one summer, except that one hadn't been made of wood, but hollowed-out bone.

"Bone Hollow," Gabe said, more to himself than to anyone else. Bone chimes, a bone hand, Bone Hollow. All those bones swirled around in his head, making him dizzy, and he gulped down a breath of fresh air, trying to calm himself. No use getting worked up now, seeing as he'd already made his choice.

He shook his head, feeling a tad more steady, and looked once again at the cottage. In addition to the glowing flowers, the stone walls and thatch roof were lit by dozens of candles of every shape and color. They were propped up on rocks and stumps, flickering away in windowsills and even nestled into the gutters. With the mist and the dark, the shadows they cast reminded him again of being underwater. Like he was back in his imaginary ocean with Gramps at his side, just waiting to see his first fish. That thought eased his mind a little more, and so he didn't jump when the girl tugged on his sleeve.

She led him to a rounded green door set in between two windows, just like something out of *The Hobbit*. The paint was cracked and peeling, but it had a cozy feel, like even the door to this cottage had been well-loved. It was the exact perfect size for the girl to fit through, which in itself was odd, seeing as she was so small. She turned a worn wooden knob in the center and walked inside without another word.

Gabe paused, but only for a moment. He could no longer hear the voices or the footsteps of his neighbors, though surely they were still out there, searching for him in the woods. He peered at the mist that clung to every inch of the valley, every tree and blade of grass. With the light reflected back on it, it looked almost solid. So maybe the girl was right and nobody could get in. The thought made Gabe feel better, but it also made him shudder. If nobody could come in, did that mean nobody could get out, either? Shaking the idea from his head, he took another deep breath and ducked through the tiny doorway.

Gabe gasped.

Wooden flutes hung from the ceiling inside, too, along with dozens of miniature candles suspended with gold string. The cottage smelled of cinnamon and honeysuckle, and nearly every free space was taken up by a stack of colorful quilts. Gabe tried to count them all, but everywhere he looked he found more, piled in corners and tucked away in hidden cubbies.

Hadn't Niko liked to quilt, too? He tried to remember, but it had all been so long ago.

"Set him down here," said the girl, spreading out a quilt on the couch; it was navy blue and dotted with gold stars. Gabe tried to imagine Miss Cleo offering the same care to Ollie, but he couldn't.

He placed Ollie gently on his side, and seeing him in the light awakened an ache deep in his belly. He didn't even have room to get angry, that was how pathetic his little dog appeared. His nose was all scrunched up the way a baby's gets when it's crying. His moaning had turned into ragged, high-pitched wails that really did sound more like a baby than a dog. He was soaked and muddy, and as Gabe had suspected, his back foot was broken.

"Where's your phone?" Gabe said. "We should call a doctor." Though he wasn't really sure about that. Ambulances would come any time of night, but what about vets? Besides, how would they ever find them, hidden away in the woods?

"Don't worry," she said. "We've got everything we need right here." She went to a tall cabinet painted in cool, seaside green and took out a roll of gauze and a bag of white powder. She set the two on the old steamer trunk she used as a coffee table and returned a few seconds later with a ceramic bowl filled with water. She moved so slow and serene, Gabe wanted to shake her and tell her to hurry up.

"You hold his head," she said, not sounding the least bit

panicked. In any other circumstance, Gabe might have taken exception to a stranger touching his dog, but this was a true emergency.

He knelt down in between the couch and the trunk, cradling Ollie's head. He kissed his nose and neck and cheeks. Ollie growled when the girl touched his leg, but having Gabe sitting by his side seemed to help. First, the girl wet a washcloth and cleaned off all the blood. She worked so quickly and tenderly; after a moment or two, Ollie hardly noticed she was there.

Next, she wrapped his back leg loosely in gauze. "You'd better hold on to him for this part," she said.

Gabe cringed as she closed both hands over Ollie's puny foot and pushed the bones back into place. Ollie yelped and growled just a little, but if old Mr. Yeats, the vet, had been the one touching his broken bones, surely he would have snapped. Besides, if he'd broke a bone on Miss Cleo's watch, she'd have made sure old Yeats put him down once and for all. It was a mean way to remember her, but it was true.

After that, making the cast was easy, though Gabe would have had no idea how to do it. Not to mention where to get the supplies. First, she added some more gauze for padding, and then she mixed up a plaster solution with the powder and the bowl of water. She found some extra-thick gauze that she cut into strips, dipped into the mixture, and wrapped around Ollie's back leg.

When she was finished, it only took a few minutes for the plaster to harden. Ollie sniffed at his new appendage and sneezed. Not once, but two or three times. Even Gabe had to laugh at that.

"Why don't I get us some tea?" said the girl, heading into the kitchen like it was just a normal night. Gabe soon heard cups clinking together and water heating up on the stove, as if fitting a cast to some stranger's dog were an everyday occurrence.

Feeling a heck of a lot better about his decision to come, Gabe released all the breath he'd been holding in and took a long look around the cottage. The whole thing was one big room glowing with candlelight. There was a living area, dining table, and kitchen all squeezed in snug. An island separated the kitchen from the living room. It was made out of logs, with a big flat stone for the top flecked with green glass.

"Where are your parents?" Gabe said. Peeking over the back of the couch, he could just get a glimpse of the girl's head as she added leaves to a sky-blue teapot. She did look a lot like Niko, but now that he thought about it, there were differences, too. Like her cheeks were higher and rounder, and her hair a shade too dark.

The girl didn't say anything for a while, and then the kettle started to sing. A moment later, she took a seat on the other side of Ollie, plunking a fancy tea tray down on top of the trunk. The tray was painted with all sorts of amazing decorations, flowers and butterflies and bats with rainbow-colored wings. The cups were fancy, too, with handles shaped like happy snakes and hand-painted scenes of the ocean, complete with whales and sparkly fish. Each cup had a curly initial on the front, applied with metallic gold paint.

"*W*?" Gabe said.

The girl blinked at the letter, biting her bottom lip.

"Is that the first letter of your name?"

She looked into Gabe's eyes, like she was just waiting for him to contradict her. When he didn't, she said, "I guess it is. *W* for Wynne."

"Oh," Gabe said, feeling stupid for ever thinking this girl could be his old friend. She did look an awful lot like Niko, though, and he remembered now about the quilts. She'd worked on them every night with her mother. Niko's parents had moved to Macomb County all the way from Bangladesh a few years before Niko was born. Niko's mom had joined the local quilting circle as a way of learning English, and it stuck. By the time Gabe knew her, they were bringing their quilts to homeless shelters and nursing homes, and even winning local prizes. He remembered the day she'd taken a sample to school for show-and-tell. It had looked kind of like the one Ollie was sitting on, blue with gold stars.

"Wynne." He rolled the name around on his tongue, trying to get a feel for it. A lot of people liked quilts, he supposed, and besides, why on earth would Niko be hiding out in the woods of Macomb County after all these years?

Wynne poured herself a cup of tea, sipping it quietly and watching him through the curlicues of steam.

"And your parents? Do they live here, too?"

Wynne shook her head.

"And how did you . . . you know?" Gabe's heart, if he still had one, beat faster in his chest. The more he looked at Wynne, the more certain he became. She wasn't just some stranger living in the woods. She was like him.

Wynne didn't answer at first. Instead, she ran her finger along the rim of her cup, observing him with curious eyes. "How did I what?"

There was no way around it. Gabe would just have to spit it out. He looked at her face again, real close, just to make sure, but there was no doubt about it. "Sorry, I don't mean to be rude or anything, but I was just wondering."

"Yes?"

"Well, I was wondering how it was you came to be . . . dead."

"Oh, that," said Wynne, but she looked delighted, her mismatched eyes glittering in the candlelight. "Very clever of you, really. How'd you guess?"

"Dunno," Gabe said, by way of being polite, but really it was the dark circles under her eyes and the way her lips and fingertips looked just a little gray at the edges. "So, how'd it happen?"

"It's a long story." Wynne added a sugar cube to her cup. "You sure you want to hear it?"

"'Course I am," Gabe said, his hand coming to rest on Ollie's back. He had a sudden feeling like maybe all this was a dream and any minute he'd wake up and find himself back at the campsite. But then he looked at Ollie's leg again, and remembered his neighbors pounding through the woods after him, and he knew it wasn't any kind of dream. A nightmare, maybe, but not the sort you could just go and wake up from.

"Nothing much to it, really," she said, tugging on the gold string in her hair. "There was a bug going around, what we used to call influenza."

"The flu, you mean?"

"That's right. There weren't any hospitals nearby, at least not for people like us."

"What do you mean?"

"You know," Wynne said, and then a long strand of hair fell over her shoulder into her tea, and it seemed to surprise her. "Anyway, the important thing is, I was gone a few days later and now here I am."

"Just like that?" Gabe said, strangely excited to find someone else like him. A few minutes ago, he was facing a lifetime alone in the woods, just him and his dog, and now all of that had changed. "But you're still here, like me. You must know why. You've gotta tell me."

For a moment, Wynne looked tired, like she wanted to say something more but didn't have the energy to do it. Then, instead of answering him, she nodded to the tray on the old steamer trunk. "You ought to have some food," she said, her face splitting into a crooked grin. "I'll have you know, that took all day to cook, so you'd better dig in while it's still hot."

Gabe's eyes drifted over to the multi-tiered tray piled high with sweets and cakes and chocolate-frosted cookies. There were ladyfingers drizzled with lemony icing and baby-size sandwiches just like Miss Cleo served once a year for the annual Ladies of the Bible luncheon, only these looked much more appetizing. Gabe was trying to decide what to eat first when he remembered about the plastic bag. He'd dropped it somewhere back in all the chaos. Not only that, but a bitter taste filled his mouth as he recalled the ordeal with Miss Cleo's famous sweet-and-savory biscuits. He couldn't very well take a bite only to spit it up again in front of Wynne.

"I think you'll find it tastes better if you try it," Wynne said, offering him half a smile. Niko used to smile like that, too, crinkling her nose and the right side of her mouth. *Nope, stop being silly*, Gabe thought, shaking his head. Niko didn't live in the middle of the woods, and she certainly wasn't dead. This had to be somebody else.

"I'm not really hungry," Gabe said, which was basically true, but that didn't mean his stomach wasn't yearning for a few of those sweets. "Besides, I've never met another dead person before. I thought I was the only one. You have to tell me everything. You have to—"

"Oh, and I almost forgot, something for Ollie," Wynne interrupted, and she nipped to the kitchen and returned a second later with a boiled egg and two strips of sizzling bacon.

Ollie perked up right away, snarfling something hilarious, before digging in to his dinner. He ended up getting bits of egg all over Wynne's nice starry blanket, but she didn't seem to mind. Besides, Ollie was good at cleaning up after himself, and soon he'd left nothing behind but a few spots dark with slobber. Gabe tried to imagine what would happen if he'd slobbered on anything of Miss Cleo's. A whupping for the both of them, that's what, and no two ways about it.

"You should eat, too," Wynne said.

Gabe was trying hard to come up with another excuse when something Wynne had said started to trouble him. Was it his imagination, or had she used Ollie's name? Only he was near certain she'd never heard him say it.

He watched her pick up a ladyfinger and take a tiny bite off the end. "I promise you'll like it," she said. "This food is extra special. Just for people like us."

"What do you mean?" Gabe said, but he thought he knew. "Like food for dead people or something?"

"Pretty much." Wynne laughed and handed him a chocolate-frosted cookie.

Gabe looked it over, top and bottom. "It doesn't look like dead people food."

"Just try it."

So he did. "Mmm, oh my gaw." That cookie tasted better than every sweet Miss Cleo had ever served all rolled into one. The chocolate was rich, like an entire chocolate ocean packed into one tiny bite, and somehow the buttery cookie underneath was still warm.

"You made these all by yourself?" Gabe said, but Wynne only smiled. His momentary worries about her knowing Ollie's name forgotten, he licked his fingers and then lifted his teacup to his lips.

He'd never much cared for tea at Miss Cleo's, since it always tasted bitter and lemony and not at all sweet, but he was a lot thirstier than he'd realized. He took a single, tentative sip. Soothing liquid spilled over his tongue. It smelled like honey, but it tasted like mint with a hint of something woodsy Gabe couldn't quite put his finger on. The minute it hit his lips, his whole body tingled with warmth, the good kind, like sitting by the fireplace on a frozen winter night.

"That's not half bad," Gabe said, grinning, and Wynne started piling his plate full of sweets.

"You'd better eat all of these," Wynne said, plopping the overflowing plate down on Gabe's lap. "We've got big plans for tomorrow. And Ollie better rest up, too." In response, Ollie kicked out his leg and snorted in his sleep.

"Sounds like you've been expecting us?" Gabe said, tightening his grip on his teacup, but just a little.

"You could say that." Offering her same playful grin,

Wynne popped up and took her cup and saucer to the kitchen. Gabe turned around slowly, not knowing what to think, but Wynne didn't go for a knife or anything nefarious. Instead, she set the dishes gently in the sink and proceeded to stare out the kitchen window for a while, like she was watching something outside that Gabe couldn't see. When she came back around to where Gabe was sitting, she surprised him once again by kissing him square on the forehead.

"You can sleep on the couch," she said, straightening up, as if kissing strange houseguests was the most natural thing in the world. "Plenty of blankets, use whichever you like best." She patted the stack of quilts piled up on the back of the cushions.

"What about you?"

Wynne's smile widened. It was sad and happy at the same time. "I think I'll get a little fresh air before I turn in." She walked over to the door and turned the knob. "Don't worry about the candles. They'll go off all by themselves. Oh, and, Gabe, I'm glad you decided to come." With that, she slipped out the door and disappeared into the mist.

CHAPTER TEN
• HOME SWEET HOME •

Gabe had never been much into prayer, on account of Miss Cleo whacking him with her Bible one too many times for falling asleep in church. Praying looked an awful lot like sleeping, so Gabe thought it safest to avoid both. But now, with Ollie snoring away by his side and the candles flickering overhead, he thought praying might not be such a bad idea after all.

"Dear Lord, if you're up there, I'm sorry to say that I'm dead. Of course, you probably knew that already. Thanks for sending Wynne to help Ollie, and me, too, I reckon. Speaking of Ollie, if you could see fit to make his leg heal up fast, I'd sure appreciate it."

Gabe squeezed his eyes even tighter, thinking hard what to say next. "I'm guessing there must be a reason why I'm still here, instead of up in the sky sitting on a cloud or whatever it is people usually do when they die." Gabe bit his lip hard, searching for the right words. "If Gramps and Mama and Daddy are up there with you, I sure would like to see them. It's been a good long while, and now that I'm dead, I figured that, you know, maybe I'd be visiting with them soon."

He sat in silence, as if waiting for an answer, but the only sounds came from the tinkling chimes outside and Ollie's sweet, honking snores.

"Well, I guess that's about all," Gabe said, hanging on a bit longer in case his answer from heaven was just a second or two delayed. Ollie grumbled and growled in his sleep, the way he sometimes did when he was dreaming about chasing squirrels. "Alright, then. I suppose I'll be signing off. Thanks again for sending Wynne to help us. Over and out."

Gramps had always taught him to end his prayers like he was using a walkie-talkie. That way it'd feel like God was right there listening on the other end. Gabe didn't know if it worked, but at least it reminded him of Gramps.

Thinking of Gramps made him sigh, and sighing made him tired, not to mention his night spent running from his former neighbors. He was about ready to call it a night when he spotted something hiding just underneath a stack of chocolate-glazed éclairs. It smelled salty and sugary at the same time. Gabe wiggled his finger underneath to find a single bacon and maple syrup biscuit, just like Miss Cleo's.

Gabe didn't know what to think, but he didn't have time to ponder, anyway, because Ollie had woken up and started to bark. "Alright, you dang spoiled hound." He peeled off a chunk of bacon and tossed it to Ollie.

To his surprise, Ollie rolled it around in his mouth and then spit it out, puckering up his lips like he'd just tasted a lemon.

"What's gotten into you?" Gabe said. He gave him a hunk of buttery biscuit instead, but Ollie turned his nose up at that just as fast. "Oh well, you dodo brain. More for me."

Gabe took his time relishing that crunchy, greasy, mapley ball of goodness. He had no idea how long it took him to eat it, but it was worth every second. And the strange thing was, even though it looked just like Miss Cleo's biscuits, it tasted even better. That was partly because of the maple that melted on his tongue and made the whole inside of his mouth tingle. But it was also partly because Miss Cleo wasn't standing right over him nagging him to stop dropping crumbs on the carpet.

Ollie, being the stubborn dog he was, kept right up with his begging. Gabe gave him a peanut, a pretzel, and a piece of shortbread cookie. He turned up his nose at each and every one.

"Oh well, your loss, you silly mutt."

He was just sticking some foil over the rest of the food when he realized what must have happened. "You think it's because this food is only for dead people?" Ollie tilted his head at Gabe, as if he was really considering. "Ain't that just about the creepiest."

But Ollie didn't seem to be much concerned with the reason, he just wanted to eat. He wiggled off the couch, despite his recent dire injury, and wobbled all the way to the kitchen on three legs, where he promptly started to howl.

"Now, aren't you something," Gabe said, shaking his head. "Who said you could get up and walk around already?" But Ollie ignored him and put on his cutest, dopiest puppy face.

Gabe sighed. "Alright, you dang ornery mutt." He followed him into the kitchen, intending to search out some scraps, when he found a boiled egg in a little plastic baggie on the countertop. It had Ollie's name on it.

"Well, I'll be danged," Gabe said, a little shiver working its way up his spine.

"Rarf, rarf, rarf!"

"Alright, alright, but you'd better eat it this time."

He gave Ollie the egg, and he gobbled it down, just like normal. Strange, that egg having Ollie's name on it, but then again, it wasn't even close to the strangest thing he'd seen that day, so he decided not to worry about it.

Once he was finished with his egg, Ollie hobbled back to the living room, crawled onto the couch, and went straight to sleep, leaving Gabe alone in the kitchen. The tile felt cool under his bare feet. He bent down and saw that each one had been painted like the squares of a quilt, all in different colors and patterns. A dozen teapots hung from hooks on the wall, in the shape of mice or cats or dragons wearing fuzzy sweaters with scarves around their necks.

Gabe wandered around the kitchen into the small nook that held a dining table but only two chairs. Everything was cozy and quaint and inviting, like the hand-knitted placemats on the dining table that read, "Why not sit and stay a while?"

Maybe it was his imagination, but it seemed like the candles in the windowsills and on the shelves had started to dwindle. Gabe peeked out through the picture window to find the moon well on its way back to earth. It would be morning soon, and he'd better try and get some sleep.

What had Wynne said about having plans for him in the morning? He scrunched up his forehead, but quickly decided he was too tired to ponder. Whatever it was would just have to wait.

He squeezed onto the couch next to Ollie, using him as a footrest this time instead of a pillow. He was careful not to touch his hurt leg, and Ollie was so tuckered he didn't so much as stir. Gabe closed his eyes, thinking it would take him a while to calm down from all the day's events, but he sank right then and there into a deep, untroubled sleep.

All around and unbeknownst to him, the candle flames dimmed and then went out one by one with tiny puffs of silvery smoke.

CHAPTER ELEVEN
• ST. CHRISTOPHER •

Gabe woke up to the sharp stench of chicken feathers. That would be on account of Miss Cleo letting those dang chickens roost in his bed. He squeezed his eyes shut, dreading the sound of pans banging together in the kitchen. That was the sign it was time to get up and muck out the coops. Worse than that, once he was done he had to sit down for one of Miss Cleo's tribulation-filled breakfasts. Tribulation because if he did one thing wrong, like slurp his grits or spill his milk, Miss Cleo would start sucking on her teeth and be downright nasty to him for the whole rest of the day.

He wasn't sure how much more he could take. It was like walking on eggshells in his very own house, and not to mention Ollie. Miss Cleo kept him chained up in the barn all night, and most of the day while Gabe was working, in the name of protecting her dumb old chickens. But that dog had never looked foul at a chicken in his whole dang life, and Miss Cleo knew it.

Cursing his luck and Miss Cleo and those stinky chickens, Gabe opened his eyes, and even as he did the smell around him started to change. Instead of chicken gunk and toe cream, his nostrils picked up the faintest scent of hot honey buns. Gabe blinked, and a pair of warm brown eyes peered down at him, and they didn't belong to any chicken. It was Ollie, and he was sitting square on Gabe's chest.

"How'd you get in here, you clever hound? Only don't let Miss Cleo catch you, 'cause she'll have your behind."

"Not today, she won't," said a voice behind him. Slowly, the rest of the room swirled back into focus, the quilts and the candles and the sea-green china cabinet. Something sizzled and popped in the background, and Gabe sat up to see Wynne in the kitchen, frying up some bacon. "Morning, sleepyhead. 'Bout time you two woke up."

Gabe was about to say something, but then Ollie's tongue attacked his mouth and nose, and it was all he could do to keep breathing. Strange, seeing as he was dead, but in that moment he was pretty sure he'd never been happier in his whole life. At least not since Mama and Daddy and Gramps had died.

"Alright, alright, that's enough, you dang pup."

"Rarf!"

Gabe lifted Ollie onto the ground, and he proceeded to wobble into the kitchen on his three good legs and start licking Wynne's ankles.

"Sorry about that; I can put him out if you want." Miss Cleo could be heard screeching halfway down the block anytime Ollie's tongue came within a foot of her skin.

Wynne, on the other hand, bent down and kissed him on the nose. "And lose my best helper? No thank you." She scooped two thick strips of bacon onto a plate, blew on them to cool them down, and set them at Ollie's feet. That dog was so darn happy, he nearly fell over from excitement.

"So where's your bedroom?" Gabe said, peering around the tiny cottage, searching for a doorway he hadn't noticed the night before. There wasn't one.

"I don't get much sleep nowadays." Wynne shrugged. She stowed the rest of the bacon in a plastic baggie and stuck it in the fridge.

"Aren't you going to have any?" Gabe said.

Wynne offered a sad smile. "Oh, that food's not for us. Ours is right behind you."

Gabe turned around to find the tray from last night, only now it was piled with buttery eggs, steaming sausages, and stacks of sugary waffles.

"How on earth?" Gabe said, taking in the wonderful, salty-sweet smells. It all looked so real. "Is it magic?"

"Definitely." Wynne picked up Ollie and came to sit beside Gabe on the couch. Ollie would usually be begging in the presence of so much delicious food, but today he just ignored it. "Here, let me show you."

"Show me what?"

"You'll see." Her eyes sparkled with excitement, despite the long shadows under her lids that looked even darker than the night before. "First step is to picture something someone else wants. It can't be for you, or the magic won't work."

As she spoke, Ollie licked underneath her chin. Miss Cleo would have clocked him one for sure if he'd tried that, but Wynne just smiled wider. "Ready? Close your eyes, go on." Gabe did as he was told. "Good, now hold out your hand and imagine something you'd like to give to someone else. It could be anything. Think about the shape, the color, the smell of it. Focus all your energy on that one thing. See if you can feel it in your hand."

Gabe did his best to focus. He thought about the shape, small and round and silver, the cool feel of it against his palm. He thought and thought, but no matter what he did his hand stayed empty. "I don't think I've got any magic."

"Nonsense, you only need to focus on the person you want the item for. Go on."

So he did, and before he knew it something cool and solid appeared in his hand. He could feel the weight of it, pressing down on his palm.

"Open your eyes."

He did, and there was his ma's old necklace, a silver St. Christopher medal on a matching silver chain. She'd left it to Gabe, or she would have if she'd made a will, but somehow it had ended up in Miss Cleo's jewelry box. It had just about burned him up the day he'd gone to church to see her wearing it. That same night, he'd snatched it back when she was busy with poultry business and hid it under his mattress.

"I want you to have it."

He held it out to Wynne, and she stared down at it for a long time, chewing on her bottom lip.

"I don't mean it romantic or nothing like that," Gabe said quickly. "Just a thank-you for saving my dog." And for making him feel at home for the first time in just about forever. He didn't know Wynne that well, true, but now that he was dead, it wasn't like he was gonna meet anyone else to give it to. Besides, he'd rather Wynne have it than nasty ol' Miss Cleo.

"No one's ever given me a present like this before," she said. "Are you sure you want me to have it?"

"'Course I'm sure."

"Okay, then."

With her fingers shaking just a little, Wynne slid the chain over her head and examined it. "It's beautiful."

"Thanks, it belonged to my ma." He didn't explain about Miss Cleo or how he was grateful to Wynne for giving him a home, but hopefully the necklace said what he couldn't.

"I know," Wynne said, and outside the wind picked up and the chimes clanked against the side of the cottage.

"What do you mean, you know?" Gabe's skin prickled.

"Come on," she said, dropping the pendant down the front of her dress. "I've got something else to show you."

CHAPTER TWELVE

· THE POND ·

Wynne picked up Ollie, who was happy for a chance to nuzzle into her neck and lick behind her earlobes, and led Gabe outside. He expected it to look different in the daylight, the way Christmas decorations seemed to lose their magic as soon as the sun came up. But Bone Hollow hadn't changed a bit. If anything, it looked better. Mist still clung to the valley, but it was clear and sparkling with sunlight. The wooden flutes tinkled in the breeze, forming a happy, woodsy tune. The blue flowers bloomed all around the cottage and down the path, only a little less bright than in the nighttime. And the valley wasn't nearly as small as he'd imagined.

The winding stone path and neatly trimmed hedges stretched on for acres, past mossy hillsides and squat, dew-covered pines.

"Come on, follow me!" Wynne said, and she took off running down the path with Ollie yapping away in her arms.

They passed cozy hollows thick with green vines and twisting, ancient bark. There were streams and gardens and a bush cut in the shape of a giant lion with sunflowers for eyes. It was all so strange and wonderful, Gabe could have spent hours examining every nook, but Wynne was running too fast.

"Hey, wait up!"

She zoomed around corners, running so swiftly along the tall hedgerows that her feet blurred and all he could see was her white dress whipping in the wind like a ghost.

"Rarf, rarf, rarf!"

Ollie was having the time of his life, by the sound of it. Wynne crossed an old wooden bridge in a single bound, and then came to a stop, fast as a lightning bolt, at the edge of a small pond. She placed Ollie gently on the ground, then plopped down onto the grass. Gabe skidded to a stop just in time. One more second and he might have run them over.

"Where are we?" Gabe said, peering around and pulling Ollie into his lap. The pond was surrounded by trees all around except for the spot where they were sitting. To his astonishment, he saw two fishing poles propped up on sticks and a tackle box full of rubber worms.

"You must fish here a lot," Gabe said.

"Nope." Wynne picked up the rod closest to her and slid a worm onto the hook. "This is my first time."

"But you've got fishing poles and everything." A thick green film covered the pond, just like the one where he and Gramps had always liked to fish.

Wynne rolled out a bit of extra line and dropped her hook in the water.

"That's not how you do it," Gabe said. "You've got to cast it, like this, so you get your hook right in the center of the pond."

Gabe showed her how to do it, but Wynne just smiled.

"You went fishing a lot, didn't you? With your gramps?"

"You gotta stop doing that," Gabe said, shivering against the chilly morning air.

"What?"

"Saying things you're not supposed to know. It's creeping me out."

That made Wynne laugh. "It's easy, you know. You should try it."

"Me?"

"Yeah, go on."

"I wouldn't know how to start."

"First, you've got to look at someone, really look at them. You can try it on Ollie if you want."

"But I already know what he's thinking." As if to confirm this, Ollie swatted Gabe's chin with one of his paws. "Hey, now, mind your manners."

"Alright, you can try it on me, then."

"You?"

"Come on." Wynne set down her pole and turned to face him. "First you have to look at me."

"Now?" Gabe said.

"Sure, why not?"

"No reason, it's just . . . maybe you could look out at the water instead."

Wynne rolled her eyes, but she shifted her body so she was facing the water. "Now pick one spot and look real hard at it. Like my earlobe or my nose."

"Or the strand of gold in your hair?"

"That'll do," said Wynne, smiling. "Now stare at that spot until your eyes start to go fuzzy around the edges. Don't blink and don't move, just let it go fuzzy. Keep on staring, that's right, and after a while . . ."

"After a while what?"

"Shhh, don't talk! You have to concentrate."

So Gabe stared hard and concentrated, until his eyes started to go fuzzy. He was about to say it wasn't working when an image appeared to him out of the fuzz. It was a girl, about Wynne's age, scrubbing out erasers in a big bucket of water. She couldn't be Wynne, though, because she looked different, with shorter hair and skin a richer shade of brown.

"What'd you see?"

But Gabe ignored her, because just then he saw another image. A woman with deep lines under her eyes and her hair pulled into a bun came around the corner. "Come on, Winifred, time for lunch. Bread and cheese and Papa's world-famous gravy."

"Did he call it that?" said the girl, drying off her hands on her apron.

"Sure did. You know your papa."

"Sure do."

They both laughed, and then the girl ran toward a small house, more like a shack, where a man with a scraggly black beard was holding out his hands, waiting for her.

Gabe would've liked to see more, but a cool breeze drifted across the pond just then, ruffling Wynne's hair and drawing him out of the vision.

Gabe blinked, wondering why the girl in Wynne's memory didn't look a thing like Wynne. "I don't understand," he said.

"My papa sure made some mighty fine gravy," Wynne said, eyes still focused on the pond. "Best in the county."

"But that wasn't you. Couldn't be." Gabe stared so hard at Wynne's face, she had no choice but to turn and look at him. How could she be one person now and another person in her memories?

"And what if it was?"

"But that old schoolhouse you were standing behind. It reminds me of the one Gramps's pa used to go to. He showed me a picture of it once, and that school was nearly eighty years old."

"Is that right?" she said, sounding amused as usual, but also a little afraid.

"And you can't be more than a year older than me, at most.

Besides," Gabe said, ignoring the sudden tugging he felt on the end of his rod, "that wasn't you. You look like . . ."

"Go on."

"Well, like my old friend, that's who."

"Your best friend." Wynne tugged on her earlobe, the same way Gabe did when he was waiting to get back his score on a test he already knew he'd failed.

"No, that was . . ." But the more Gabe thought about it, the more he realized Wynne was right. Niko might have moved away in third grade, but at least she'd always been there for him. Even after Mama and Daddy passed on, she'd never once laughed at him when he cried. That was more than he could say for Chance. He'd once called Gabe a sissy in front of everyone in class, even Maisy Hughes, and all because he'd refused to help Chance shove a raccoon down old Mr. Benton's well. "Now that you mention it, I suppose she was my best friend."

"I thought so."

"Hang on," Gabe said, wild thoughts racing through his head. "What're you trying to tell me? You're not . . . I mean . . . you're not really Niko, are you? She's not dead?"

Wynne laughed, looking the slightest bit relieved. "Definitely not, at least as far as I know. She moved to California, didn't she?"

"Yeah, but . . . you do look like her."

"About that." Lazy clouds drifted by overhead, scattering the sunlight sparkling on the surface of the pond. Wynne smiled, that same strange but familiar smile, just like Niko's. Gabe looked at her, right in the eyes this time, and as he did her smile faltered.

"Don't be mad," she said. "I was trying to be helpful, I swear."

"Why would I be mad?" To his surprise, Gabe noticed his heart beating in his chest, so fast it was hard to believe he was dead. A fresh breeze blew in across the pond, shaking pine needles from the trees into Wynne's hair. Then, as the breeze fell quiet, Wynne started to change.

Her skin, once a cool earthy brown, like the ground just after a thaw, grew warm and rich, like Gramps's legendary caramel paprika hot chocolate. Her eyes started to glitter, the hazel one especially, and the next thing he knew they weren't grass green or soft brown anymore but a deep gray, flecked with black.

Gabe's mouth dropped open real slow as her loose strands of hair slithered up her back like tiny snakes and wrapped into tight braids atop her head. The braids glowed in the sunlight, almost like a crown. Her dress stayed the same, though it looked older somehow, the lace worn and fraying at the edges, just like the dress the girl had been wearing in Wynne's memory.

In fact, she looked exactly like that girl now, even down to the round chin and pointy nose and sly, good-humored smile.

"Well, I'll be danged," Gabe said, by way of response. "If you could look like anybody, why'd you go around pretending to be my best friend?"

"I wasn't pretending, exactly," Wynne said, her smile fading away altogether. "I just didn't want to scare you."

"Sure is a funny way to go about it," Gabe said, but to his surprise he found that he wasn't scared, not really. If Wynne could create delicious food out of nowhere, then why couldn't she change her shape? "This is the real you, though, isn't it?"

"'Course it is. You saw for yourself, didn't you?"

"I guess." Gabe pulled Ollie a little tighter to his chest. "Can you change into anyone? Living or dead?"

"Just about," she said, but even as she did her eyes drifted up over the treetops and her smile faded. "I can show you tomorrow, if you want."

"What about today?" Gabe watched as Wynne stood up and shook the dirt from her dress, never taking her eyes off the treetops. "What is it?" he said. "What do you see?"

Wynne took a long time answering. Gabe stared and stared at the spot where she was looking. Once, he thought he saw something, too, kind of like a shimmering fog floating below the clouds, but then it disappeared and he figured he must have imagined it.

"You've been gone all night. You can't leave again," Gabe said, and now he did feel afraid. Not because of Wynne changing shape, but because he didn't want her to leave him, too, like everybody else in his life.

Finally, Wynne pulled her eyes away from the sky and

looked at Gabe. "That'll be for me, I'm afraid. I wish I could stay longer, but I don't think this one can wait."

"This what?" Gabe said.

"Don't worry, I'll tell you all about it later."

"How long will you be gone?" Gabe stood up, too. It felt strange to want Wynne to stay so badly, but now that he'd found a friend, he didn't want to let her go.

"Don't worry about me," she said, her smile brightening. "I'll be back as soon as I can."

"Rarf!" Ollie jumped on Wynne's knees and did his darndest to lick her elbows. Apart from still wearing his cast, you'd never know he was a bona fide invalid.

"Are you sure we can't go with you?" Gabe said. His cheeks burned with embarrassment, but he didn't much care. "We can help, we can—"

"Bye now." Wynne flushed as she met his eyes, though maybe it was just the wind making her skin go pink. "Oh, and when you're heading back, make sure to follow the path."

"Wait," Gabe said, but just then a harsh gust shook the treetops, ruffling Wynne's hair and whipping her dress around her legs. She winked, and the next thing he knew, she was turning so fast she might as well have swallowed a twister. A sharp clap shook the air; Wynne waved and a moment later she was gone.

CHAPTER THIRTEEN
· THE PATH ·

Despite his hurt leg, Ollie leapt up and snapped the air in the spot where Wynne had been.

"Ain't that something," Gabe said, in a voice barely above a whisper. Being dead sure was a lot different than being alive. He stood there blinking for a good long while before finally coming back to his senses.

"Come on over here, you ornery mutt. Sit down by me before you hurt yourself." Gabe dragged Ollie by his side, and after a lot of coaxing, he settled down with his head resting on Gabe's belly. "That's more like it."

He watched blue-and-green dragonflies skim the pond for a while, trying to piece together everything that had happened. He liked the way the sun shimmered off their wings, almost like they were made of glass. He liked the way the pond smelled, too. Like algae and rock and freshly turned mud. His old fishing hole smelled just the same way, the one he always went to with Gramps.

Gabe rubbed his temples, thinking hard, but he couldn't

make sense of a single thing that had happened. He knew one fact for certain, though. Being dead wasn't all that bad. In fact, it was just about the only good thing that had happened to him since Gramps had passed. No more mucking out chicken coops or cringing every time Miss Cleo walked into the room. No more feeling like a stranger in someone else's house. Wynne wanted him here, and Ollie, too. Even if she was a mite more mysterious than he would have liked. Still, Bone Hollow was more home to him than home had ever been, and he'd only been there a single day.

The only thing better would have been seeing Mama and Daddy and Gramps, but now that he was dead, maybe Wynne could help him with that, too. She must know other dead people, or how to get to them.

"Isn't that right?" Gabe said to Ollie, but Ollie was already snoring. Gabe took it as a sign, dropping his head down onto the warm grass and closing his eyes. He didn't intend to nod off, but the next thing he knew a familiar smell prickled in his nostrils.

The smell was fresh-cut grass and wood and cigar smoke. Bengay and newspaper and starched polyester pants. In other words, it was Gramps.

Gabe opened his eyes to a blinding golden light.

"Hey-ho, Captain. Thought I might check in on you."

Gabe blinked and there was Gramps, sitting right next to him holding a fishing pole. He wore a light blue sweater and darker blue pants. On his head was the visor Gabe had bought him, the one with "#1 Gramps" stitched on the front.

"I'm real sorry about all this," he said, and as he did a chill breeze ruffled the thin strands of gray hair poking out of his ears. "I suppose you're lucky," Gramps said, though his eyes looked sad. "It's a big responsibility, but I know you can do it. I'll be waiting for you, Gabe, remember that. Me and Mama and Daddy."

"Why can't I go with you now?" Gabe said. "I'm dead, Gramps. Just like you. You can take me with you."

Gramps shook his head. "Not yet, Captain, but don't you be afraid, you hear? Remember what I always say?"

"But why not?" Gabe said stubbornly. "I'm grateful for Wynne and all, but she's not my own flesh and blood. If I could just see you for a little bit, spend time with you, I—"

"One day." Gramps smiled. "Be patient. Listen."

"To the ocean?" Gabe said. "I don't want to listen. I want—"

"That's right, the ocean. 'Cause it's been around a heck of a lot longer than you." Something tugged on the end of Gramps's line and he started to laugh. "Well, what do you know!" He reeled it in and stared at the thing dangling from his hook. It wasn't a fish at all, but a moldy old cloak made of black velvet. "I reckon that's for you," Gramps said. "What should we do with it?"

"Throw it back," Gabe said, looking closer. It was crawling with hairy spiders and cockroaches as big as half-dollars.

"You sure?" Gramps looked at Gabe with that same sadness twinkling in his eyes.

"'Course I am. Hurry up, they'll get on you."

Gramps tossed it back, and it splatted in the dirty green water.

"I'll be waiting for you, as long as it takes." He stood up, every one of his bones creaking and cracking. "Remember, don't be afraid. Promise?"

Gabe tried to stand up, too, but he'd gotten tangled in his fishing line. "Wait, Gramps, don't go! Tell me how I can find you!"

"Promise me, now. Promise you won't be afraid."

"Sure, I promise, but hang on a sec." He struggled against the thick plastic wire, but it was no use. It had come alive somehow and was coiling tightly around his arms and ankles. "Please, take me with you!"

"Goodbye, Captain. And remember what I said. I'll be waiting."

Gabe reached out, but it was too late. The golden light exploded with another snap and Gramps was gone. A moment later, something wet and slippery crawled across Gabe's face. He sat up with a start, only to find Ollie sitting on his chest again, covering his face in slobber.

He pulled him off gently, gasping hard to catch his breath. He didn't know whether his dream had been real or just another nightmare, but he was sure glad Ollie had woken him up.

"Better head back to the house," he said. "It's already starting to get dark."

And it was. Not totally dark, but the sun had dropped behind the trees, bathing everything in burnt orange light.

"Come on, I'll carry you," Gabe said, but Ollie wasn't listening. He took off on his three good legs, like having a broken bone was nothing more than a minor inconvenience. "Wait for me!"

They jogged down the winding path together, noticing things neither had seen the first time past. Like a fountain in the shape of a whale spurting sea-blue water. Around another bend they found a boulder coated in furry green moss. Only it wasn't really a boulder, because, as Gabe watched, it began to move. A head poked out, so old and rough it was hard to believe it hadn't been carved from rock. Two lamplight eyes blinked at them in the dying sun, and then, very slowly, the giant tortoise turned around and slid into the waters of a shadowy marsh.

Gabe reached for Ollie, trying to pick him up, but he shot ahead, leaving Gabe no choice but to follow.

"Stay on the path," he said, but Ollie wasn't listening. He disappeared into the center of a hedge and started barking.

Heart clenched in his chest, Gabe pushed his way through the scratchy bush into a clearing bathed in eerie blue light. The smell of dust mixed with rotten meat filled the thick air around them. A figure stepped from behind a tree stump, bending down to grin at his dog. Only it wasn't like any grin Gabe had ever seen. For one thing, it stretched all the way to the man's ears. For another, there was something inside his mouth that looked an awful lot like a small bird. It squeaked and flapped its wings to get out, but the man's long, thin teeth held it trapped inside, like bars.

"Come on, Ollie, get away from there."

Ollie's barking had gone quiet, and he stood still, as if petrified, staring up at the long, thin man that wasn't really a man at all. He didn't have any feet, for starters. Just legs that stretched out like taffy and ended in sharp points. Every time the wind blew, he rippled, which wasn't surprising, seeing as Gabe could see clean through his body to the trees on the other side.

"That's right," the man was saying in a voice like a swollen, dead tongue. "Come to Pappy. He'll take care of you."

He curled his gloved finger in Ollie's direction, and it was so long it wound around itself five times before stopping. Ollie didn't move.

"Come 'ere, sweetie. Pappy doesn't bite. Not anymore he doesn't." The man leaned closer, his torso bending and stretching. He sucked his lips at Ollie, and the bird in his mouth squealed and tore at his teeth with its claws.

"You leave him alone!" Gabe cried.

He reached for Ollie, but the man was too fast. His middle finger shot out like a tongue and coiled around Gabe's ankle. It was so wet and cold Gabe's skin ached.

"Get off!" He kicked out, and the long, impossible finger

cracked. At the sound, Ollie finally sprung into action, growling and snapping at the broken finger as it shot back into the man's hand.

"Ollie, no!" Gabe shouted as Ollie got snatched up in the man's waiting arms.

"That's a sweetie pie," the man said, a string of yellow drool dribbling down his chin. "You're my sweetie now!"

A sharp wind shook the hollow and drew the man and Ollie back toward the darkness of the trees. Gabe knew he had to act fast.

"Give him back!" he said. For the second time in his life, he aimed a punch square at the man's swollen face. To his surprise, his head flopped over as soon as his fist struck, like his neck was filled with rubber instead of bone. It bounced back and proceeded to ricochet to and fro as if on a spring.

His stretchy arms squeezed tighter around Ollie, but Ollie wasn't having any of that. He sank his teeth into the man's flesh, just above the elbow, and scrambled free.

"Oh dearie me, how rude!" said the man, patting the place where Ollie had bitten him. Instead of blood, there was just a hole where Ollie's teeth had sunk in, and a gray space not far behind, like looking into a punctured balloon. And like a balloon, he began to whistle, his arms shriveling up one by one, until they were nothing but empty flaps of wrinkled skin.

His legs flailed and his head beat against his shoulders in the building wind.

"Let's get out of here," Gabe said. Ollie barked in agreement, and together they ran for the hedges.

They had almost made it when the pointy tip of a leg pierced Gabe in the back. He cried out in pain and fell hard to the grass. Ollie seized the leg, tearing at it with his teeth, but it broke free, slithering around Gabe's stomach.

The violent gust that was sucking the man-thing back into the shadows grew stronger. He was hardly a man anymore, just a frayed piece of bubble gum flapping on the wind. Gabe clawed at the grass, trying to squirm free of the man's grip, but it was no use.

"Help me," Gabe gasped. Ollie grabbed hold of Gabe's T-shirt and dragged him as hard as he could toward the hedges. Only problem was, the leg wouldn't let go and that wind was sucking the man as hard as it could back into darkness.

"No!" he cried as the wind picked up, tearing him free from Ollie's teeth. Next thing he knew, he was careening across the grass toward the gnarled trees and the cold, stinking blackness that lay beyond.

CHAPTER FOURTEEN

• THE TUNNEL •

"That's about enough!" cried a voice from somewhere in the maelstrom. Just like that, the wind stopped, the man-thing snapped back into the shadows, more like a rubber band than a person, and a hand closed around Gabe's shoulder.

"I see you met our resident spook," said Wynne, offering him a tired smile. "Or at least, one of them. I thought I told you to keep to the path."

"What was that thing?" Gabe spluttered.

"I'll explain inside," Wynne said, ruffling Ollie's hair with a sigh. His poor mutt was shaking something awful. "Come on, and this time don't go running off."

No sooner had they all three sat down on the sofa than Wynne produced a steaming mug of hot chocolate from behind Gabe's left ear. "Drink up, it'll help with the shock."

Not surprised to find that he, too, was shaking, Gabe took a sip of steaming hot chocolate. It tasted just like the kind Gramps used to make, with dark chocolate and caramel and a hint of paprika. Warmth oozed down his spine into each of his limbs. Even Ollie, who was sitting in his lap, stopped shivering.

"But what was that thing?" Gabe said again, after downing half of his mug.

"Oh, that," Wynne said, her eyes looking more tired than ever. "You see, Bone Hollow isn't like other places. The world is different here. More . . . wobbly."

"Wobbly?"

"Exactly, and sometimes things get through."

"From where?"

Wynne shrugged, like getting attacked by stretchy ghosts with birds in their mouths was no big deal and Gabe should just get over it. "Not sure. Over there, I suppose. You know, the other side or whatever people call it. But don't worry, they can't hurt you."

"Wait a minute here, the other side? Like *h-e-l-l* other side?"

"Not exactly." Wynne nudged Gabe's mug closer to his mouth. "Have another sip, it'll make you feel better."

"Well, if it's not *h-e-l-l*, then what do you call it?"

"I don't know, I've never really given it a name."

"What about the Dead Place?" Gabe said, an old memory bobbing suddenly to the surface of his mind.

"What's that?" Wynne smiled, amused.

"Nothing, really. It's just this place Gramps made up that was full of goblins and ghasts and people with giant wings like crows. He used to tell me all sorts of stories about it when I was little."

"The Dead Place, huh? I suppose it's something like that, but like I said, they can't hurt you."

"Are you sure?" Gabe remembered the pain of that pointy leg piercing his skin, but when he looked, there was no mark, not even a single red spot.

"They're not really here, you know? It's more like they're peeking, slipping through the cracks a little, but they can't actually do any harm."

"If you say so," Gabe said, downing the rest of his hot chocolate in a single gulp. He had to admit it did make him feel better, like his whole body was wrapped in a fuzzy winter sweater.

They sat in silence while Wynne sipped quietly on her hot chocolate. After a bit, she went into the kitchen to make boiled eggs for Ollie, and Gabe couldn't help turning around and watching her as she worked.

He concentrated, hard, and after a while he was back at the old schoolhouse. "Millard Colored School," said the hand-painted sign above the doorway. Wynne was out back, kicking a tin can against the wall. She wasn't wearing her white dress anymore, but a dark gray wool coat and lace-up boots to match.

Gabe stood right beside her as she kicked the can over and over. She looked at him once, but her eyes drifted through him to the doorway of the school beyond. The door had opened and people in gray and black suits filed out. The last to come was the woman Gabe had seen before, with her hair swept up in a tight bun. He guessed it was her mom. She placed an arm around Wynne's shoulders and pulled her into a hug.

"He's in a better place now, sweet girl."

"Leave me alone."

"Sure you don't want to come in and say goodbye?"

Wynne wriggled out of her grasp and ran. Away from the schoolhouse and the crowd of people in black.

A cracking eggshell brought Gabe out of Wynne's memory. She was watching him now, a sad look on her face. He thought about asking her about what he'd seen, but he decided she already looked sad enough for one night.

Wynne brought the egg over to Ollie and he ate it out of her hands. When he was done, she wiped her hands on a dishtowel and went to stare out the dining room window.

"What is it? What are you looking at?"

Gabe strained his eyes, seeing nothing at first but waves of mist reflecting back the moonlight. But then, over the trees and far away, he glimpsed a faint blue flicker. Then, the harder he looked, the brighter it grew, till it wasn't a flicker anymore, but a giant flame roaring over the treetops.

"Something's on fire," he said. "We should call the fire department."

Wynne smiled, but the smile didn't reach her eyes. "It's not that kind of flame."

"What is it, then?"

"I can show you, if you like."

Gabe hesitated. "Is that where you went yesterday, too?"

Wynne didn't answer. Instead, she set down her cup and turned to Ollie. "You'll have to stay, boy. Your leg isn't ready for a big adventure."

But Ollie yipped and wiggled his bottom with such vigor that Gabe had no choice but to take him.

"Come on," Wynne said. "It's best if we start outside."

"How are we going to get there?" Gabe said. "It looks awful far away."

"Take my hand."

But Gabe's hands were occupied with holding Ollie, so Wynne grasped his elbows instead.

"Now close your eyes and picture the flame."

"You mean we're going to get transported or something, like in *Star Trek*?"

Wynne blinked a few times, like she didn't understand.

"You know, the TV show?"

"Just concentrate. Think of nothing but the blue flame. How it moves back and forth on the wind. Imagine it calling to you, begging you to come near. Hold that in your thoughts, the brightness of it, the flickering. Let it draw you in."

A silence stretched between them. Gabe tried to focus, but after a while he couldn't help himself.

"Nothing's happening. I think I'm doing it wrong."

"Open your eyes."

Gabe would have screamed, but he was pretty sure he'd just swallowed his tongue. They were zooming through a tunnel made of swirling gray clouds. Ollie had his mouth open and was doing his best to capture wisps of cloud on his tongue.

"What's that?" Gabe cried as a face emerged from the churning mass of gray. It had bulging eyes, droopy ears, and a nose like a deflated balloon.

"Going somewhere?" said the face, dissolving in a fit of laughter.

"Where are we?" Gabe gripped Ollie tighter to his chest.

"Ghost tunnel," Wynne called over the roar of the wind. "Don't worry, they won't hurt you."

"They?" Gabe peered around at the gray walls rushing past, and sure enough he caught sight of other faces, some pleasant, others foul, and more than a few pointing transparent fingers at him as he went.

The tunnel veered sharply to the right and then down. Gabe's stomach shot into his chest. Wynne squeezed his elbow harder and Ollie yipped and howled in excitement.

"Next time, maybe we should walk!" Gabe shouted, but just then a plump ghost shot into the tunnel, bouncing off Gabe's chest.

"Apologies!" he warbled, but it was too late.

The jolt had separated him from Wynne.

"Gabe!" she cried, but it was no use. He dropped out of the

tunnel into the cold night air. Free-falling at top speed, Ollie clawing at his chest and neck. In less than a second, he burst through the clouds and the ground sped toward him. He held on to Ollie with all his might, the wind trying like mad to tear him away.

Then, without the slightest warning, he plunged into blackness and Ollie flew from his arms.

CHAPTER FIFTEEN
· SHADY OAKS ·

The next thing he knew, someone was setting him down gently on the grass. He turned around to see a kindly old friar with a bald head and a very tiny pair of silver spectacles smiling at him. Ollie came down next, carried in the arms of the plump ghost, who wore an apron and a pair of fluffy plaid slippers. He placed Ollie in Gabe's arms, but he soon jumped out and kept trying to kiss each of the ghosts in turn. The problem was he kept falling through them, right to the other side.

"Apologies again," said the plump ghost in his quivering, friendly voice. "I always do get in the way."

"Nonsense," said the friar, giving the other ghost's arm a reassuring pat. "The lad must learn how to focus."

"But he's new. He wasn't to know."

"True enough, true enough. I say!" He turned his attention to Ollie. "Do you mind? That tickles!" He shivered, his transparent body rippling like water. The next time Ollie went to lick him, he banged his nose into the friar's shin.

"It's not as easy as it looks, remaining solid," the plump ghost confided. "I'll never understand how you lot manage it."

"He's not a ghost, now is he?" said the friar reasonably. "Anyway, we had best be off. No use distracting the boy from his work."

"Work?" Gabe said.

"Nice to meet you," said the plump ghost, waving. "Ta-ta!"

Together they zipped up and up and in a few seconds were indistinguishable from the gathering rain clouds.

"What on earth was that?" Gabe said, pulling Ollie into his arms again and planting a kiss square on his forehead. For his part, Ollie seemed unfazed by their near escape from doom. "And more importantly, how are we gonna find Wynne?"

As if in response, Ollie barked at something moving above the treetops up ahead. It was the blue flame, and it was even bigger and wilder than before.

"Come on," Gabe said, plucking up his courage. "Wynne might need our help."

Gabe picked Ollie up, and they raced through the trees, the air humid and electric against their skin, the way it always got just before a storm. Soon they reached a deserted country road. On the other side stood a tall iron gate. The flame was so large now it cast a blue light over the entire landscape.

Gabe and Ollie crossed the road. A rusty sign hanging from an old rope on the front of the gate read, "Shady Oaks: May All Who Enter Be at Rest." The gate stood open, and even before he stepped through, Gabe could see it was a cemetery.

Headstones stretched back as far as the eye could see. Flat ones and thick ones, marble and plain concrete. Statues of lions and generals stood guard atop some of the most elaborate graves. Gabe and Ollie walked in silence down a narrow gravel path, their breath leaving traces of white on the air despite the heat.

The blue light overhead cast strange shadows that crept over the grass toward them. The farther they walked down the path, the larger the graves became, until each one looked like a tiny stone house at least as big as Miss Cleo's old shed. He thought these ones were called mausoleums.

Gabe opened his mouth, thinking he might shout Wynne's name, but it didn't seem right somehow to be shouting in a graveyard. He let his mouth fall shut again, and simply followed the flame in silence.

Finally, at the very back of the cemetery, Gabe saw someone. He stopped dead and watched. It wasn't Wynne, just an old man sitting in a lawn chair next to an open mausoleum. He was talking to someone, though Gabe couldn't see who, and his teeth were chattering.

"Put the Christmas lights up last week, Maud, just the way you like 'em. Blue and gold on the front, and green for the tree. It's hard to get the star on top nowadays, without you to hold the ladder, but I had the Smith boy come over and do it. Nice kid, he'll be ten years old come the end of December."

He paused, and he poured himself a cup of something hot from a metal thermos. His hands were shaking so bad he spilled most of it onto the grass.

"Guess you don't know the Smith boy. You went and left us the month before he was born." He was quiet for a while, and when he spoke again his voice sounded scratchy. "Ten years is a long time, old gal. But I did like you said, I kept going." He took a ceramic mug from a bag by his feet and poured another cup of steamy liquid. This one he set on the steps leading down into the mausoleum.

"I think I'm coming home to see you soon," he said, both crying and laughing when he said it. "And, you know what, it's about damn time."

Just then, a figure emerged from behind the statue of an angel with a sword and two massive wings. It was Wynne, only she seemed taller somehow, and thinner. She walked toward the old man, and as she did her shape started to change. Her skin pulled tight against her face. So tight he could see her jawbones jutting out from underneath. Her hair grew long, draping over her shoulders and down her back, until he blinked and it became a cloak, flapping on the humid wind.

The man turned around slowly and stood up. The cloak covered Wynne's body now and hung low over her eyes. She reached a hand out toward the man, and her fingers were made of long, thin bone.

"Maud," the old man said, choking on his tears. "You came."

He walked toward her, and for just a moment Gabe saw what the old man must have seen. A plump woman with straight gray hair wearing a pale pink jogging suit, tears spilling down her cheeks. He took her hand, except the golden light filtering through the trees shifted, and it wasn't Maud or Wynne, it was a skeleton.

They walked together over the sparkling grass, only the old man didn't leave any footprints. Gabe looked again at the lawn chair. The old man was still there, clutching his chest. The thermos had fallen from his hand, and brown liquid stained his pants. But, despite all that, he was smiling.

When Gabe turned around again, the light disappeared with a snap and there was Wynne. A look of relief registered on her face, and she took a step toward him. Gabe took a step back.

"Stay right there," he said, breathing hard, the wet air filling up his lungs. "Ollie, no!"

Ollie, being a stubborn hound, refused to listen. He wiggled out of Gabe's arms and bounded across the grass toward Wynne. Only she wasn't Wynne, not really. Her body flickered like the channels on Gabe's old TV set. One second she was Wynne, frail and thin in her worn white dress, the next she was a skeleton, tall and horrible and draped in black.

"Leave him alone!" Gabe sprinted across the grass and sprung, wrestling Ollie to the ground. Ollie, not a fan of having a good kiss interrupted, howled in protest.

"Who are you?" Gabe said, backing so far away he could barely see Wynne's face without the light from the blue flame.

"I think you know."

Gabe shook his head. "No way, it can't be. Why? Why did you come and find me?"

"Don't be scared, Gabe. It's not what you think. You saw so yourself."

"I don't know what I saw. Just tell me who you are!" Gabe squeezed Ollie so tight he yipped, but Gabe hardly even noticed. "Tell me!"

"I'm Death."

Ollie slid from Gabe's arms onto the grass. He looked from Gabe to Wynne and back again.

"Shut up," Gabe said, barely able to speak above a whisper. "You're not, you can't be—"

"I am." She stepped into a faint sliver of moonlight. She was Wynne again, at least for the moment, and her crown of braids glittered in the pale light. "And, if we're being totally honest, so are you. That is, if you want to be."

Gabe dropped to the grass, too, as if in slow motion, as if his legs couldn't hold him up anymore. Everything that had happened with Gramps and the cloak raced around inside his head, fighting for attention. Wynne wasn't going to bring him to see Mama and Daddy and Gramps. How could she? She was the one who'd taken them away.

"But how?" Gabe said. "You're not Death. You're just a kid."

Wynne started to answer, but then she too fell to her knees. She looked tired, like Gramps that time he'd raced Gabe all the way around the Bentons' farm. Only more so, a deep-down tired that stretched all the way to her bones.

"I won't be around forever, you know." Wynne smiled, but Gabe just kept on shaking his head.

"You're out of your dang mind, that's what you are. I don't know what you did to that old man, and I don't wanna know. But if you really are Death . . . if you . . ." Sensing Gabe's anger, Ollie tried to crawl into his lap, but Gabe stood up instead, cheeks burning. "Death took Mama and Daddy and Gramps from me. If you think for one dang second . . ." And then a certainty dropped down on him from above, like an anvil crushing his chest under its weight. "It was you."

"What was me?" Her usually serene expression grew troubled.

"You killed my parents."

"No, Gabe, you don't understand." Wynne tried to get up, but her legs were shaking so bad they wouldn't support her. She looked like Wynne again, but Gabe knew better.

"You killed that man, and you killed Mama and Daddy, too. And Gramps!" Here he was, thanking God for sending Wynne to save him, when she hadn't. She was the reason he was all alone. Heck, she was probably the reason he was dead.

"No, I promise, I didn't." She reached for him, sounding truly desperate, but Gabe pulled away. "Let me explain. Let me . . ."

But it was too late. Gabe took off running, ignoring the rain that started falling from the sky, making dark lines down the back of his T-shirt. Maybe it was a coincidence, and maybe it wasn't, but the second Gabe set foot on that torn-up country road, a pair of headlights blazed around the bend. A horn blared in Gabe's ears, tires screeched, and the air erupted with a crack!

CHAPTER SIXTEEN
· INTO THE WOODS ·

Gabe fell back hard on the asphalt, tumbling over Ollie and whacking his head on a rock. He was certain he'd been run over. Near frantic, he felt his chest and legs, only to find that his body hadn't been flattened after all. He sat up slowly and saw an old pickup truck peeling off down the road, sending a spray of gravel in its wake.

Slowly, he pulled himself to his feet, wiping pebbles and tar off his already beat-up jeans. That was when a horrible thought dropped to the pit of Gabe's stomach. "Ollie? Where are you, boy?"

Before Gabe could get up and search, that dang hound bounded out of the shadows and started flapping his tongue, licking the dirt and muck from Gabe's fingers. "Thank the Lord!" he said, kissing that dog about fifty times on the head. "Don't you ever scare me like that again! Not ever!"

He held Ollie even tighter and cursed those dang taillights as they disappeared around a bend and out of sight. A sick feeling worked its way up the back of his throat, and even though

Ollie was fine and he hadn't been flattened like a pancake the way he'd thought, he threw up on the side of the road. Nothing came out except for spit, but it still made his tummy ache something awful.

"Dang!" he shouted, pounding his fist into the dirt. "Why does everybody have to be such a gosh dang liar!" He peered back across the road, through the open gate leading into Shady Oaks Cemetery, but only for a second. Not that he wanted Wynne to follow, not anymore, but it sure had been nice to have a friend.

"This is goodbye, then," he said to his former friend, swallowing the bitter taste filling up his mouth. And to think he'd given her Mama's St. Christopher medal. With a sigh, he picked up Ollie and crossed the road into the dark, wet forest. Fat droplets of water showered his head as he walked, but Gabe ignored them. Ollie writhed and squirmed in his arms, but the second he put him down he took off running back toward the cemetery. Finally, Gabe gave up and hoisted that silly dog over his shoulder, despite his howling.

"She's no good," Gabe said as they walked. "She's a liar and a killer, too. That's the only reason she saved us. To turn me into a monster just like her."

When Gabe reached the field where they'd fallen out of the sky, the shower turned into a full-on storm. He ran toward a large swath of trees that seemed to go on forever in every direction. He had no idea if he was heading toward Bone Hollow or away from it, but in that moment he didn't much care. It just felt good to run. To shake up all the confusion and anger eating away at his chest.

He'd had a home, a real home for once, and Wynne had to go and ruin it. Warm rain splashed down his face and pooled in the pockets of his jeans. The ground grew soggier as he ran, and before long his feet were caked in mud. The air stunk of mold and soggy tree bark, and Ollie's whine grew so pathetic Gabe had no choice but to put him on his three good paws.

"You stay with me, now, promise? I can't lose you, too."

Ollie gave him a solemn look, which was about as close to a promise as a dog could get. They ran together till Ollie was soaked through and shivering. At the first hint of thunder, he planted himself on Gabe's feet and refused to keep going.

"Guess we'd better find a place to spend the night," Gabe said, but the whipping rain filled up his mouth and nose, drowning out his words.

Ollie stuck close to Gabe's heels now as they trudged through the storm, searching for a cave or a hollowed-out tree or somewhere else to hide in. But Very, Very Tall Hill was nowhere in sight, and when Ollie took off for the safety of an old pine tree, Gabe had no choice but to follow.

They huddled together on a bed of sopping pine needles. Ollie curled up on Gabe's lap, shaking, his eyes wide and frightened, and nothing Gabe said would calm him down. That poor mutt always got the same way during a storm, like the whole sky was falling down around him.

Just like the night Gabe had found him. Or, to be more accurate, the night Ollie had found Gabe. A storm had been raging over Macomb County like nothing anyone had ever seen, even the old-timers. Three tornadoes had touched down in the space of a minute. Gabe had left the safety of the storm shelter on Miss Cleo's urging in order to fetch her poultry competition scrapbook from inside the house. That was when he heard something howling and whining underneath the floorboards. The house had a crawl space, and Gabe had to go down there every few weeks to empty the rat traps or scare out a misbehaving possum, but this didn't sound like any possum he'd ever heard.

Ignoring Miss Cleo, whose wails could be heard all the way across the yard, Gabe left the scrapbook inside and crawled up underneath the house. He couldn't see what was making the noise at first, but it sounded so dang pathetic his heart just about broke. Then he fished his flashlight from his pocket and the beam lit on a skeleton of a dog, bald except for a few tufts of wiry brown hair.

It took Gabe nearly an hour to coax him out of his hiding place, and by then the storms had just about passed. Miss Cleo was so mad at Gabe for putting her precious poultry memories at risk that she locked him out of the house. Gabe spent the night in the storm shelter, curled up on Gramps's old army cot, that bag of bones he called a dog snoring in his arms.

They'd been best friends ever since that night, but Ollie had never gotten over his fear of storms. "Don't worry now, you just try and get some sleep. Things'll look better in the morning."

Gabe said it, even though he didn't really believe it. How could things look better in the morning when the only friend he had in the world, apart from Ollie, that is, had betrayed him? Here he was, thinking he'd found a home, a place where people wouldn't turn him out or treat him like dirt, and in the end it had all been a trick. Wynne was only being nice because she wanted something from him. The whole thing, the warm, cozy couch, the trays full of food, the pond and the candles that went off all by themselves, it was nothing more than a lie.

Death had taken everything he'd ever loved, and now Death had taken away his home, too.

He still couldn't believe that Wynne had hurt that man, but he didn't know what else to think. Wynne was Death, she'd said so herself, and that meant he'd stay as far away from her as possible, no matter how wet and how miserable he got.

Ollie kept right on shaking all through that night and into the next morning. He didn't fall asleep until the sun had risen, casting pale golden rays on the still-wet leaves. Despite the ache in his bottom, Gabe couldn't get up for fear of waking

Ollie. He drew in a deep breath, and soon he fell asleep, too, mouth open, head leaning against the cool, calloused bark.

When he woke up again, he wasn't in the woods anymore. He was in Gramps's old log cabin, sitting on the scratchy wooden floor right by Gramps's bed. Gramps was coughing something terrible. He didn't look at all like Gabe remembered. His skin hung loose around his eyes and his mouth was sunken in like someone had plucked out all his teeth.

"What's wrong?" Gabe said.

Gramps coughed some more and then he closed his eyes and pressed his hands together, and Gabe knew he must be praying. He didn't pray out loud, the way Gabe did, though, and after about a minute his hands fell limp by his sides.

Gabe leapt to his feet and tried to shake Gramps awake, but it was no use. Gabe had turned into a ghost, chilly and see-through and gray. He swiped his arm right through the center of Gramps's chest, but he didn't move, not a single inch. That was when Gabe saw the date circled on Gramps's Trees of Macomb County calendar. September 14, the same day Gramps had died.

He'd died in his cabin all alone, and no one had even found him till three days later, on account of Miss Cleo refusing to drive Gabe over for a visit. Of all the things Miss Cleo had done, that was by far the worst. Gabe had never told anyone, except for Ollie, but those three days haunted him long after

Gramps was gone. Sure, he was dead, but it still wasn't right for him to be left all alone, even if he didn't know it.

Looking at Gramps made Gabe's knees go all shaky, and he sat down hard on the edge of the bed. He wanted to wait with him, like he hadn't been able to the first time, but just then the door creaked open and a figure walked in.

"You!" Gabe said, but the thing in the black cloak didn't hear him.

"Nice to see you, Captain," said the stranger, giving Gramps's shoulder a little shake. "Been a mighty long time, but I told you I'd be back." The black cloak faded, and instead of Wynne, Gabe saw a young woman in a smart gray suit. Her blond hair curled around her head like a halo, and she was smiling so wide Gabe couldn't help but smile, too. Something about her looked familiar, but Gabe didn't know for sure till Gramps climbed out of bed and spun her around in his arms.

"Well, I never," he said, laughing, standing up straighter than Gabe had ever seen him. "Sure took you long enough."

"That it did," said Gabe's very own gran, and to Gabe's extreme discomfort she planted a kiss smack-dab on Gramps's lips. "Now I'm back, and there'll be no more moping around in bed all day. I've got plans, mister."

Gramps was too busy laughing and smiling to answer.

"Come on, now. What do you say we get you home? Last I remember, you promised me a night out. Unless you're too tired?"

"Tired! You've got to be kidding. I feel like dancing!"

"That's more like it." She wrapped an arm around his shoulders and together they walked out the door into the yard.

"Hang on," Gramps said. "I can't go yet." He scanned the dirty patch of grass, with its rusty car parts and broken washer and dryer, like he was searching for something.

"He'll be fine," she said, and just then, with the sunlight shining in her hair, Gabe thought she was the most beautiful person he'd ever seen, even if she had died before he was born. "After all, he's got someone to look after him."

"If you mean that old bean sprout Miss Cleo, I wouldn't be so sure. I never should have let her take him in, even if I was a little under the weather. Maybe I should have a word with her before I go, just to set her straight."

"Now, Captain, you know she did her best," Gran said, taking his arm and leading him toward a bright orange light. "But caring for a child isn't the same as caring for a chicken."

"Exactly! No boy should have to spend all day mucking out the coops. I have half a mind to—"

"You'll shush up and follow instructions, that's what you'll do," Gran said, tightening her grip on his arm. "Besides, I'm not talking about Miss Cleo, you silly old coot. I'm talking about Ollie."

"Ollie's a dog!" Gramps snorted.

"Exactly. Who better?"

After mulling the matter over for a while longer, Gramps

reluctantly followed Gran's lead. They walked together into the blinding waves of light, and Gramps only looked back once. Gabe watched them go, and when Gramps looked back, Gabe waved, even though he knew Gramps couldn't see him. They looked so happy, but then, just like that, he remembered. The realization flooded over him like a tsunami crashing into shore. The person holding Gramps's hand wasn't really Gran at all.

"No!" Gabe ran and threw his arms around Gramps's waist, but it was too late. The light disappeared with a snap and Gramps was gone.

Ollie was barking at him when he woke up for real, covered in pine needles and soaked from head to toe. "What is it?"

Gabe shot a nervous glance around the woods, wondering if Wynne might have followed him. She did have her ghost tunnel or whatever it was, but the woods stood silent in the bright afternoon sun.

"How long did we sleep?" Gabe said, shaking the awful dream from his mind. Ollie bounded over and offered Gabe a quick smooch on the mouth. After giving every one of his muscles a good stretch, Ollie still hadn't stopped barking and wiggling his tail.

"What's gotten into you?" Gabe said, and then he realized it might have something to do with his rumbling tummy. The tiniest bit of doubt crept into Gabe's mind at his decision to leave Bone Hollow behind, but it was gone almost as soon as it had started. People survived in the woods all the time, at least they did in stories. If they could do it, surely he could find enough food to feed one puny dog.

"Come on, you, time to go hunting." Gabe pulled himself up despite the ache deep in his bones.

Hunting turned out to be a lot harder and messier than Gabe had anticipated. For one thing, they hardly saw any animals in the woods, and the ones they did see were mostly mice. Ollie might be hungry, but not hungry enough to go chomping down on something so sharp and insignificant. Second, Gabe kept slipping and smearing his already filthy jeans with mud. By the time the sun sank down in the sky, both Gabe and Ollie were slopped from head to toe in muck, and they weren't any closer to finding something Ollie could eat.

At least it wasn't raining, so they lay down in a grassy, moonlit clearing. "Don't worry, boy, we'll have more luck tomorrow."

But Gabe was worried, and not just about his poor pup going hungry. Gabe watched as, overhead, the stars revealed themselves one by one, until there were hundreds and then thousands of them blinking down on him in a giant web of light. They reminded him of tiny fish flitting to and fro in the deepest part of the ocean. Not that he'd ever been there, but the way Gramps always talked about it, it was almost like he had. He was always telling Gabe interesting facts about the ocean, too, like how 95 percent of it was still undiscovered. Imagine an entire world down there that humans didn't even know about. And not just small things, either, but mammoth creatures, like giant squid with tentacles over thirty feet long.

Maybe, Gabe thought, as a chilly breeze ruffled his hair, the regular world was like that, too. Everybody thinking they know everything that goes on when really they don't. What they can see is just the surface, but dip your head under, just a little, and . . .

Gabe shivered. He pulled Ollie close to his chest, but Ollie wasn't in the mood for cuddling. He stayed awake most of the night eating grass and then throwing it up again.

"It's only been one day," Gabe said, rubbing the scruff on the back of Ollie's neck. "We'll find food tomorrow, don't you worry."

Ollie spent most of the next day sniffing for squirrels, but not a single one dared venture out thanks to a fresh round of rain. Gabe found a pond and caught a toad and two fish with his bare hands, but Ollie refused to eat either one. It rained most of the next day, too, and by the time it was done raining, it was far too muddy to hunt. By the fourth day, Ollie was so tuckered out and weak, he hardly wanted to get up at all. Gabe left him resting in the shade of an old oak tree, panting and half-heartedly gnawing on whatever grass he could reach.

"Please, Lord," Gabe said as he searched the field for any signs of life. "Let me find something my dog can eat. It doesn't have to be a squirrel, either. A possum would do, or—"

Gabe stopped dead in his tracks. Something had disturbed the tall grass up ahead. Every muscle in his body tensed as he got ready to pounce. A normal Gabe wouldn't have a chance against a squirrel, but Gabe wasn't normal, not anymore. That same strange energy coursed through his veins. He waited and waited, and then, when the creature relaxed and went back to nibbling grass, he pounced.

He flew six feet in a single bound, and then another six, and then, with a whoop of triumph, his hands closed around something warm and squirming. It was a rabbit, not much bigger than a kitten, with pale brown fur and wide eyes dancing with fright.

"Ollie!" Gabe called, his heart pounding in his throat, or at least that's what it felt like. "Come over here."

He didn't know why, but he was finding it harder and harder to catch his breath. Ollie pulled himself to his feet and trundled over slowly, as if measuring each step. The rabbit kicked its legs and spasmed in Gabe's fingers.

"It's gonna be okay," he found himself saying to the rabbit. "Don't be scared."

Ollie trotted closer, just a few feet away now. The rabbit's struggle grew more frantic. Gabe tried to whisper more soothing words, but his mouth had gone dry. Ollie spotted the rabbit and Gabe tensed. He closed his eyes, waiting for something horrible to happen. A squeal or a crunch or a hungry growl as Ollie charged after his prey.

Instead, a wet nose touched Gabe's hand. He opened his eyes to find Ollie licking the rabbit's nose, and then bowing, bottom in the air, ready to play. With a cool rush of relief, Gabe let the rabbit go. Ollie bounded after it for a few feet, dragging his yellow cast behind him, and then flopped down once again in the long grass and went to sleep.

Gabe didn't have time to dwell on his failure or the dire nature of his situation, because just then a slew of storm clouds rolled in overhead. Despite it being first thing in the morning, the sky turned black and a cold wind rustled the dry blades of grass.

"Come on, boy, follow me," Gabe said, but it was clear that Ollie wasn't prepared to stand up for anything, even a coming storm.

Determined to find a better shelter than the underside of a tree, Gabe hoisted Ollie into his arms and headed farther into the woods. The rain picked up a few minutes later, soaking his mud-caked jeans and cutting jagged rivers down his face. Ollie yelped and cried in alarm the faster they went, but Gabe couldn't stop now. He leapt over fallen logs ripe with insects and fuzzy black mold. He scaled streams in a single bound and scrabbled up slippery hillsides still holding Ollie steady in his arms.

His heart jumped in his chest as he saw a giant rock jutting out of the earth up ahead. He ran for it, and as soon as he reached it, a long crack of thunder split open the sky, so loud the trees all around him shook. Ollie jolted with fright, as water and leaves splattered down on their heads from up above.

"Shh, buddy, you're alright. We're almost there," he said, but just then, another crack of thunder, even louder than the first, tore through the air, echoing off the rock. Suddenly, a strange tightness tingled in Gabe's left arm. Before he had time to register what had caused it, Ollie clawed free of Gabe's grasp, scrambled to the ground, and took off running, cast and all.

Fear lit up Gabe's spine. "Ollie, no, come back!" His dog had bit him, his very own dog.

Gabe was quick, especially now that he was dead, but that thunder had put the fear of God in his poor, pitiful pooch. He darted back and forth through the trees, running just as fast on three legs as he usually did on four. Gabe did his best to follow, but Ollie's black behind was barely visible against the dark underbrush.

"Ollie!"

The wind whipped Gabe's hair into his eyes, but he ran after that bounding bottom, ignoring the bark scraping his skin and the branches slapping him so hard in the face his teeth rattled. The rain blew in, even harder than the night they'd left, and it carried tiny ice chips that pricked Gabe's neck and cheeks.

"You stop right this second!"

But Ollie was having none of that. With his hair wild and wet and spiky, he tore through the thick weeds heading straight toward a creek. The creek had overrun its banks, probably due to all that rain, and water surged over the sharp rocks underneath. Before Gabe could yell, Ollie leapt.

No doubt he meant to clear the creek in a single bound just like Gabe, but he was small, on the outside if not on the inside, and he still had a bum back leg. He wiped out on the rocks, and a sharp pain shot through Gabe's insides at the sight of it. Mud splatted under his cracked feet as he ran. He watched Ollie's legs get tangled underneath him, his cast dragging him into the rushing water.

"I'm here, I got you!"

Coughing and scrabbling, Gabe reached the water. He reached for Ollie and somehow managed to push him to the other side. The sharp rocks bit into Gabe's skin as he climbed the last few feet to safety. Water beat against his ankles, and just as he was about to step onto the shore, he slipped, splashing into the raging water. Ollie yipped and growled in alarm. His eyes opened wide, all the hair rising on his back.

"It's okay, boy, see? I'm fine."

Ollie didn't seem to hear him. He looked up into the sky, like he saw some kind of monster swooping down overhead. Then, without warning, he dug his teeth into Gabe's sleeve and started to pull.

"Hey, now, what's got into you?" Gabe said, in the most calming voice he could manage under the circumstances, but Ollie kept right on tugging, digging his legs into the grass to get more traction. "Okay, okay, I'm coming."

Gabe crawled over the rocks, and finally his hands pressed down into the soft mud on the other side of the creek. He started to stand up when the branches overhead creaked, a deep groaning sound that made Gabe's nerves prickle. Ollie growled and dragged Gabe with even more fury, but just then his sleeve ripped. Ollie went sprawling back on the grass and a black shape swung down from the treetops, hitting Gabe's skull with a thud.

CHAPTER SEVENTEEN

• LOST AND FOUND •

The next thing Gabe knew, something scratchy and with far too many legs was crawling across his nose.

"Get off!" He swiped at his face, and the slimy, scratchy, crawly thing plunked into the water flowing all around him. "Why am I all wet?" Gabe thought, or said. He was still so groggy it was hard to tell which.

Slowly, he sat up and squinted into the darkness. The only light came from a thin slice of moon peeking through the tree-tops. That moon reminded him of one of Miss Cleo's yellow toenails, the kind she always left lying around on the carpet. "What happened to me?" Gabe said. Then a dull ache sprung to life on the side of his head. He rubbed it and looked around some more. Chunks of yellow plaster littered the creek bed, along with soggy strips of gauze. Gabe's eyes widened, and just like that he remembered.

The storm, the branch crashing down toward him, and Ollie nearly drowning trying to cross this very same stream.

"Ollie!" Gabe called out, coughing up mouthfuls of water as he did. "Ollie, where are you?"

Gabe listened. The wind was quiet now, but the roar of crickets and frogs and other nighttime beasts nearly drowned out his words.

"Ollie!" He pulled himself free of the muck and started to run. It was no use searching for tracks, since that dang moonlight was too pale and sickly to reach the ground. Besides, Gabe couldn't have stopped to examine tracks even if he'd wanted to; his heart was thumping too hard and fast to allow it. Maybe it wasn't pumping blood, 'cause how could it? But it was pumping all the same.

"I'll find you, boy, don't worry!"

So Gabe ran, banging into trees and cutting his feet on thorns and brambles. Over and over again, he called Ollie's name, his heart swelling to the size of a balloon in his chest when he got no answer.

"Why don't you just hush up so I can hear!" he shouted at the crickets and the frogs, and lo and behold, there was a moment of quiet. As if the hordes of crawling creatures could feel the panic radiating from Gabe's small, bony chest. In the silence that followed, Gabe listened for any sign of his dog. "Ollie!" he cried, and his voice carried through the woods. Surely, if Ollie were nearby, he would hear. Seconds ticked by, and then just as Gabe was about to call out again, a fresh round of thunder shook the treetops.

All the normal nighttime sounds returned, louder than before, followed by sheets of rain. The warm droplets pelted Gabe's face and ran down the back of his shirt. In that moment, Gabe felt worse than he had in his whole entire life. Even worse than the day he'd died trying to save that dang chicken. Worse than losing Mama and Daddy and Gramps, because protecting Ollie was up to him.

He thought about sinking down into that mud and never getting up again, but that wouldn't help find his dog. So despite the fear and hurt weighing down his gut, he started off again into the darkness, calling Ollie's name. As he ran, the black trees darting past, he remembered another night racing through the woods, panic swelling up inside him.

He'd been away at summer camp, and Miss Cleo, being Miss Cleo, had left Ollie out in a storm. That poor dog'd been so scared silly, he'd gone and hidden in a drainage pipe out behind the Bentons' farm. Nobody could convince him to come out, not even Gramps, that's how terrified he was.

Finally, Gramps'd had to drive Gabe all the way home from Arkansas to rescue that poor ol' pup. The whole car ride, panic had been building up in his chest so big he was surprised he didn't explode.

"Ollie!" Gabe cried again, more frightened than he'd ever been, even on that car ride back from Arkansas. "Come out, buddy, it's okay!"

The wind and rain and shadows ate up all his words.

He had no light and no tracking skills and no idea where Ollie had gone. He could be anywhere, injured or caught in a trap or worse.

"Ollie, please come back!"

Just then, the rain turned to hard pellets the size of golf balls that plunked off the tree trunks.

"Awoo!" A shrill cry cut through the beating hail.

It was Ollie, it had to be, and he sounded hurt. Gabe followed the sound, running wild and blind, barely feeling the hard balls of ice strike his face.

"Please, Lord, if you're really up there, help me find my dog. I'll do anything you want. I'll pray every night and read my Bible and everything, Lord. Please, please, please!"

Gabe ran and prayed for what seemed like hours, not getting any closer to finding his dog, until finally a faint, silvery light appeared up ahead.

As if by magic, the storm seemed to subside the closer he got to the light. The air grew cooler and the sticky humidity was replaced by droplets of silver mist. Everything in the woods went quiet, or at least that's how it seemed. Even the leaves grew still, and not a single wing beat. Gabe stepped closer, his run slowed to a dazed walk.

Surely, it couldn't be. He couldn't have run around for days only to end up in the place where he'd started. But it was.

A tinkling music drifted on the air. Clink, clink, clink. Gabe smiled. And tears, impossible tears, streamed down his cheeks out of pure relief. Because mixed in with the eerie music was another sound. A happy barking coming from beyond the next row of trees.

Gabe stepped out of the shadows into the cool light of Bone Hollow. And even though he was scared and he hated Death more than he ever had, he couldn't help laughing. There was Ollie, huddled up in Wynne's arms, grinning and yapping and kissing her face as fast as he could.

And she didn't look scary, not anymore. Her rich brown hair sparkled in the moonlight, like it was set with hundreds of tiny diamonds instead of raindrops. She was laughing, a weak, friendly sort of laughter, like someone who hadn't had a good laugh in a very long time.

A few days ago, Gabe would have shivered and turned right back around, after snatching his dog, that is. But if he knew one thing, it was that Ollie had never come to anyone besides him in a storm, not even his very own gramps, and Gramps was the person Gabe had trusted more than anyone in the whole entire world. Wynne might be strange and mysterious and a little scary, but if Ollie trusted her more than Gramps, then she couldn't be bad. She just couldn't.

Wynne spotted him before he'd even peeked out from the trees. She offered him a sad but relieved smile, and then Ollie must have sniffed him, too, because he bounded through the trees and into his arms. His cast was gone, of course, but his leg looked better than Gabe had expected. The skin covering the wound had already closed up, and he wasn't even running on three legs anymore. There *was* something strange about the way he moved, or was it the way he looked? And who had ever seen a broken leg heal so fast? Gabe scrunched up his forehead, trying to figure it out, but then Ollie started licking inside his ears, and he decided it didn't matter. As long as he had Ollie back, everything would be alright.

"I love you, boy. I'm so glad you're okay."

Ollie was glad, too, because he wiggled and slurped and generally loved on Gabe as hard as a dog could.

"You came back," Wynne said quietly as Gabe crossed the grass toward her, Ollie licking happily at his ankles. "I wasn't sure you would."

"I wasn't sure, either." Gabe stared at his muddy bare feet, trying to think of something to say. The truth was, he wasn't only happy to have his dog back. He was happy to be here, in Bone Hollow. It felt like home, even after everything that had happened. Gathering up his courage, Gabe made himself look Wynne straight in the eyes. "I know you didn't kill that man . . . Did you?"

He held his breath, waiting for Wynne to answer.

"No, silly, of course I didn't."

"I didn't think so." Relief washed over him, and he smiled for the first time in days.

They stood for a moment in silence.

"This doesn't change anything, though. I'm not . . . I can't be what you want me to be." Living in Bone Hollow was one thing, but taking someone away to the other side, even if it wasn't technically killing, was something else altogether. "I believe you didn't hurt that man, but I can't be like you. I won't."

Wynne didn't answer, but her cheeks had gone the color of ash.

"It must get lonely out here," Gabe said. "Living in the woods all by yourself."

"But now I've got you." Wynne's lips flickered into a tentative smile. "You will stay, won't you? At least for a while."

Gabe looked down at Ollie, who was full of energy again, chasing his tail round and round, like the past few days had never happened. He wouldn't stay forever, and he wouldn't be like Wynne, but it sure felt good to be home. "For a while," he said, unable to stop himself from smiling.

"I'm so glad you're back," Wynne said. She took his hand, and Gabe found that she was blushing. She didn't seem to notice the drizzling rain that dripped down her cheeks and onto her dress. "How about some hot chocolate?"

Gabe didn't know if he was making the right decision, but it sure felt right. Besides, at Wynne's words, Ollie bounded across the grass and straight through the front door of Wynne's cottage. "I guess that's a yes."

Wynne laughed. The musical sound tinkled in Gabe's ears. "Thank you," she said, squeezing his hand.

"For what?"

She didn't answer. Ollie barked at them from inside the house, darting back and forth from the doorway to the kitchen.

"I guess we'd better go inside," said Gabe, rain dribbling down his nose, into his mouth.

"Last one there's a pickled egg," Wynne said, and together they ran for the candlelit cottage, leaving behind the fog and the shadows and the dwindling bands of rain.

CHAPTER EIGHTEEN
• ROAST BEEF •

The hot chocolate tasted even better than it had before. Gabe and Wynne sat on the porch swing, holding their mugs in one hand and rubbing Ollie's belly with the other. For his part, Gabe was pretty sure Ollie had never been so happy in his whole doggie life. Two people giving him a belly rub at the exact same time was just about too much for him to handle.

"I owe you an explanation," Wynne said, staring intently at her mug.

Gabe watched the steam drifting off the top of his hot chocolate.

"It's been so long since I was your age, I guess I forgot what a shock it would be."

Gabe looked into Wynne's eyes and saw an old type of weariness there, like the kind Gramps sometimes wore after a hard day's work. Only, seeing that look on a face as young as hers was something different altogether. It made him sad.

"How old are you, anyway?" Gabe said. "How long have you been . . ."

"Too old," she said, fixing her eyes back on her mug. "I should have told you right away, I know that now." She drew in a deep breath, and Gabe had an inkling she might start to cry. "I never was very good at getting things right. Even way back when."

"I'm sure that's not true," Gabe said, and Ollie settled his head on Wynne's lap.

"Thanks." She smiled, rubbing Ollie's chin. "That helps."

The flutes chimed overhead, sending a spray of chilly water onto Gabe's toes. "And how did you become . . . you know . . . Death?"

"Oh." She drew in a sharp breath. "We don't have to talk about that now, if you don't want."

"I think I need to know." He was here, after all, instead of floating in the clouds somewhere, and he needed to understand why.

Wynne blew on her hot chocolate awhile before answering. "I died, like you. Only . . ."

"You weren't really dead?"

"Exactly." Wynne smiled into her mug. "Anyway, after a few days I got up again and just kept going. Mama and Papa hid me in the cellar, to keep me away from prying eyes, but I couldn't stay hidden down there forever."

"What'd you do?"

"One night, real late, Mama heard a tapping on the back door. She didn't dare open it, fearing one of the neighbors had discovered my secret, but then we all heard this voice calling through the keyhole. 'Open up now,' it said. 'Don't leave your old granny out in the cold.' Well, Granny was Mama's gran, not mine, and she'd died before I was born. Mama opened up the door, hands shaking, but sure enough she recognized Granny and ran into her arms."

"But it wasn't Granny, was it?" Gabe said, remembering how Wynne had looked like Niko the first time they'd met.

"No, it was. And she told Mama and Papa how I had to go with her, for good, and how they wouldn't be seeing me again. They took an awful lot of convincing, but finally they understood."

"And you?"

"Oh, I was kicking and screaming most of the way, but as soon as I saw Bone Hollow, I knew it couldn't be all that bad."

Gabe finished his hot chocolate, wishing he had about ten more glasses. He sighed, and when he looked down at his mug again it was filled to the top with bubbling hot liquid.

"I think I know what you mean." He held the mug close to his lips, letting the steam warm his face. No matter how scared he got, how much he didn't understand, Bone Hollow still felt like home.

"So your granny was Death, too, then," Gabe said, trying to wrap his mind around it. "And what exactly does Death do?"

"Sometimes, when things die, they need a little help moving on."

"Help? What kind of help?"

"Not much," Wynne said. "Just a nudge in the right direction."

"And you can do that? Give 'em a nudge, I mean?"

Wynne nodded, turning her sparkling, silvery eyes on him. "But don't worry. No one can force you to become Death; not even Gran could have done that. You have to decide for yourself."

Gabe thought that over, listening to the last droplets of rain sprinkling the awning overhead.

"I really am glad you're back," Wynne said, her eyes lingering on Gabe's. Just then, in the moonlight, he didn't think he'd seen anyone's eyes look more tired or lonely or relieved. He was just wondering how so many emotions could live in one person all at the same time when her eyes drifted to the treetops and Gabe saw a yellow flame burning in the distance.

"Is that for you?" Gabe said.

Wynne nodded slowly, setting her mug on the ground.

"You be good," she said to Ollie, kissing his head and letting him slobber a little on her chin.

She got up shakily and stood there for a while gaining her balance.

"Maybe you should stay and drink some more hot chocolate," Gabe said, watching how her thin body swayed back and forth in the wind.

"I'll feel better in the morning." She offered a weak smile. "Now you two get some rest. You've had a long night."

"What about you?" Gabe said, but Wynne was already walking away.

Ollie leapt up and followed her across the yard, doing his best to herd her heels, like they were nothing but skinny, naked sheep. Wynne laughed, if you could call it that, and then she said, "Dinner's in the kitchen."

"But . . ."

Gabe was about to offer his assistance, but he couldn't force the words out of his mouth. Even though he could tell she needed his help, and he knew she wasn't hurting anyone, not really. He just couldn't. Death was still his enemy, even now.

Wynne didn't spin around or disappear in a cloud of smoke. She just trudged up the hill separating Bone Hollow from the rest of the woods, moving as if each step took every ounce of her energy.

"You'll be here when I get back?" she said, turning around at the top of the hill, her dress pale in the moonlight.

"You can count on it," he said, and he meant every word. Wynne was strange and confusing and a little creepy, but the judgment of a good dog was more than enough for him. Besides, Bone Hollow was his home, at least for a little while.

So, Gabe and Ollie went inside, and he found a tray of all his favorite foods sitting on the kitchen counter. Roast beef and ham, spicy chicken strips and double jalapeño pizza with pepperoni on the side.

He hadn't even realized he'd been hungry till he saw all that delicious food. He took the tray into the living room and set it on the steamer trunk. Before he gorged himself like he had the night he'd arrived at Bone Hollow, he at least stopped long enough to say his prayers. He had no idea if you still had to pray once you were dead, but he figured it couldn't hurt.

"Dear Lord, if you're up there, thanks again for saving my dog. I don't know about all this Death stuff, but I reckon Wynne is one of yours either way."

Gabe could hear Ollie snarfling while he was supposed to be taking a moment of silence.

"What are you doing?" Gabe snapped his eyes open, only to find Ollie halfway through a giant slice of roast beef.

"You can't eat that food, you dang hound. Remember what Wynne said. That food's only for dead people."

But Ollie gobbled it up and then sat there wiggling his bottom, an innocent look on his face. Gabe felt Ollie's forehead, just to make sure, but he seemed alive and well to him. "Don't be silly," he said aloud to himself. "There must be something different about this food, that's all."

So they chowed down together, and when the tray was empty, they curled up on the sofa and went to sleep, the candles overhead flickering with soft yellow light. Wynne didn't return home the next morning or the next afternoon. A fresh tray of food appeared on the old steamer trunk around lunchtime, and though he was worried about Wynne, both he and Ollie had their fill.

When they were finished, they decided to go outside and check the grounds. The cool mist tickled Gabe's nose, and Ollie kept sneezing and then wiggling his bottom so much he started turning in circles. Gabe thought about going to look for Wynne over by where the flame had been, but seeing as she'd probably used the ghost tunnel, it would be impossible to find her. Instead, he decided to wait for her by the pond.

He fashioned a lead for Ollie out of an old bit of rope he found behind the cottage. He tied it around Ollie's belly instead of his neck, so he wouldn't choke, and off they went to find the pond. The path looked much the same as it had a few days before, but not exactly. Gabe was almost certain that some of the trees had switched places. Flowers that had only stood a few inches high towered almost as tall as Gabe's head. And the nook where the tall man had nearly kidnapped Ollie was overgrown with bloodred roses, their long stems thick with thorns.

"This might be harder than I thought," Gabe said, but no sooner had he said it than he turned a corner and there was the pond, sitting peaceful and still, just the way he remembered it.

Gabe sat down, and Ollie climbed into his lap. There were still two fishing poles, and he picked up his and cast the rubber worm into the water. He sat there fishing for a while, rubbing Ollie's bottom and his tummy and his long, thin nose. He didn't catch anything, and after a while his lids started to droop under the late-afternoon sun. He was just about to drift off to sleep when he saw Gramps's face floating behind his eyes. He didn't think it was a dream, since he could still feel the cool breeze on his face, but he could see Gramps, too, lying in his sickbed. He could see how he coughed, and the look on his face when Wynne—Gran—walked into the room. He wasn't scared, not the way Gabe had expected him to be, and he definitely wasn't alone.

Gabe shook off the pull of sleep, and when he blinked, there was someone sitting next to him.

"You sure do sleep a lot," she said, her eyes twinkling. She looked just about more tired than anyone Gabe had ever seen, her gray eyes sinking back in her skull and her hands shaking from the effort it took to sit up.

"What took you so long?" Gabe said, touching his fingers to a braid that had come loose near the back of her head. The hair there was streaked with gray.

"That happens sometimes, getting lost, I mean. Besides, there was more than one flame."

"How many?"

"Four."

"All at the same time?"

Wynne nodded, and then she slumped back on the grass and closed her eyes. "I think I need a little rest. Just for a few minutes."

"Let me help you back to the house," Gabe said, but she was already gone, dead to the world. Using the skills Wynne had taught him, Gabe conjured up a pillow and placed it gently under her head.

He tried to stay awake, to make sure Wynne was really okay, but with her snoozing next to him and Ollie snoring away on his lap, he slowly let his body drop to the grass. Despite his best efforts, he drifted off to the soft rustling of leaves and the gentle whisper of wind rippling across the pond.

CHAPTER NINETEEN

• HIDE-AND-SEEK •

When Gabe woke up, sunlight spilled across his face and he was pretty sure he was drowning.

"Okay, okay, I'm awake," he spluttered, pushing Ollie and his slobbery tongue off him. Ollie loved to lick inside his mouth and nostrils every morning. It was one of their not-so-fun rituals.

"How are you feeling?" Gabe said, but Wynne was gone. He searched the skyline for any sign of a flame but didn't find one. Maybe it was too far away. "I hope she's okay," he said aloud, and he did. Even if he didn't understand why she had to do what she did. Not really.

A chilly breeze blew in across the pond, ruffling Gabe's shirt. He peeked down at the wound on his stomach, except it wasn't a wound anymore. It didn't even look like a second belly button, just a small purple pinprick, not even big enough to call itself a mole.

Gabe felt around on his back, and that side had healed up, too. As if that tornado and that weather vane and that gosh dang chicken had never even existed. And maybe it was a little like Miss Cleo had never existed, too. She hadn't been very kind or very friendly, but Gabe had to admit he was a little sad at the thought of never seeing her again. A little, but not a lot.

Ollie set about licking Gabe's belly clean, paying extra attention to his used-to-be hole. While he was distracted, Gabe took the opportunity to reexamine Ollie's leg. It had healed, too. The swelling was gone, and the hair around the wound had even grown back. It was a dang near miracle.

"What do you think about that?" Gabe said.

Ollie answered by slobbering his face one last time, and then barking and wiggling his tail in excitement.

"Alright, already. We'll go find Wynne. Who knows, maybe she's back at the cottage making breakfast."

Together, Gabe and Ollie headed back to the cottage, finding the pathway through the garden had changed once again. The tall hedgerows that lined the paths, turning the garden into a sort of maze, kept moving. At least, they must have moved, because each twist and turn looked different than it had the day before.

They passed a row of tall purple plants with petals like mouths. Ollie went up to sniff one, and it snapped half-heartedly at his bottom. Sticking closer to Gabe's ankles, Ollie wound through ivy-covered arches and rosebushes full of plump buds the size of cantaloupes, with Gabe close on his tail. Finally, they came upon a small window of branches, climbed through, and emerged in Wynne's front yard.

"That's some garden," Gabe said as an extra-chilly breeze lifted up his hair. He was just sliding off Ollie's new leash when a voice nearby got his attention.

"Over here," said the voice, or maybe it was the wind.

"Did you hear that?"

Ollie barked in response, and then Gabe heard the wispy voice again.

"Other way."

Gabe spun around. "Wynne?"

The air stood still for a moment, and then a fresh breeze whizzed past his ear. "What are you waiting for? Come and find me!"

Ollie barked and sniffed and then took off running into the mist, and Gabe had no choice but to follow.

"Getting closer," Wynne said, her voice like a spring breeze flitting over his shoulder.

He turned and slapped the air, but there was nobody. Then Ollie tensed up, and his tail started wagging, and he leapt. "What's gotten into you?" Gabe said, but before he could finish, a pair of thin arms materialized out of nowhere to catch his dog.

Ollie barked and slobbered the air, and Wynne started to appear. She showed up in sections, first her neck, then her chest, then her legs. Every time the wind blew it revealed another part of her.

"You found me," she said once she was well and truly there. Her smile shone a little brighter than the night before, and Gabe couldn't help but smile back. "Now it's your turn to hide."

"Hide? Why?" Gabe said.

"Hide-and-seek, obviously."

Wynne took a seat in the grass, pulling Ollie into her lap. The mist cleared around her, like it knew she was sitting there and wanted to make sure Gabe could see. She looked much less tired than earlier, and she was smiling again. "The first step is to forget about your skin," she said, as if it were the most normal thing in the world. "Come on, sit down over here. Close your eyes, too, at least until you get the hang of it."

Gabe sat down and closed his eyes. "But why?"

"Shush, you'll see."

"And how, exactly, am I supposed to forget my skin?"

"It helps to think about the wind. At least, it did for me, back when I was still learning. The important part is to imagine the breeze covering every inch of your body, snaking around your ankles and falling over your shoulders like a cloak. A see-through cloak made of air and sky and nothing at all."

"If you say so," Gabe said, but already his body felt different. Lighter, as if Wynne's words had a magic touch that could make him disappear.

He focused on the air blowing over him, washing everything solid away like the rush of ocean currents. Picturing the ocean always made him relax and forget everything around him, and it worked even better than he'd expected. His body swayed slowly back and forth in rhythm with the waves.

"You can open your eyes now," Wynne said, a good deal later.

Gabe opened his eyes. When he looked down at his body, he smiled so wide he almost spoiled the effect.

"I'm invisible," he said, holding out his arms and waving his hands. Except, his arms and hands weren't there. There was nothing where his body had been except for air and trees and grass.

"You're hiding," Wynne said.

And he noticed she was looking at him, but not in the eye. He waved a hand in front of her face and she didn't even flinch.

"This isn't hide-and-seek," Gabe said. "It's magic." And he couldn't help but laugh. He looked down and his body flickered in and out of focus. The laughter was ruining the illusion, but it didn't really matter. Ollie squeezed out of Wynne's arms and jumped into Gabe's lap. His focus faltered and just like that the illusion collapsed. He fell back onto the grass laughing harder than ever.

They practiced hide-and-seek for the rest of the afternoon, even though Wynne was still tired, so she mostly just watched and gave instructions. Hiding in plain sight was a lot harder than it sounded. It required pure focus, for one thing, and Gabe's mind had a tendency to wander. Ollie licking him and jumping on him all the time didn't help matters much, either, but Gabe couldn't get mad at him for being a good dog.

"You'll get better at it," Wynne said when the sun started to fall in the sky and the air turned cold.

She stood, her gaze falling on something burning far away on the horizon.

"Do you have to go?" Gabe said, realizing they'd been sitting there together the entire day. They hadn't even eaten.

Wynne nodded. "They need me." She stood up, though it took her a long time. Her eyelids drooped, and she was shaking so much Gabe was afraid the wind might knock her over. He'd been having so much fun, he hadn't noticed her strength starting to wane.

"Maybe you should stay home, just for tonight," Gabe said, ready to catch her if she fell. "You look like you need some rest." Who would've thought Death could be so weak and frail?

Wynne smiled, and then walked away. She disappeared into the woods without saying goodbye.

That night, he and Ollie slept on the sofa, surrounded by quilts and flickering candles. When he opened his eyes again, he was back in the old cabin with Gramps. Gramps coughed and stared at the door like he kept expecting Gran to walk through, only this time she never came. He waited and waited, and after a while, Gramps sat up even though his body stayed behind.

"It's alright," Gabe said. "Gran'll be here soon." And he found himself hoping she would come, even though he knew it was really Wynne and he knew that her coming meant Gramps would leave him behind for good. But Gramps looked so sad and lonely and scared. Somebody had to come. They had to.

CHAPTER TWENTY

· WINIFRED WIST ·

Wynne didn't come back the next morning. Gabe fed Ollie some scrambled eggs from the tray, then stood on the cool kitchen tile with a puzzled look on his face. Strange as it sounded, the cottage had changed since the last time he'd seen it, too. The quilts looked thinner, more faded somehow, as if whatever magic had created them was starting to wane. The back garden visible through the kitchen window had become overgrown with vines, the blue flowers closed up, their petals wrinkled and wilting.

With nothing much to do but wait for Wynne, Gabe decided to fill a teapot with cool water and see if a drink might help the flowers bloom. Ollie followed on his heels as he wound around the garden path.

He drizzled the sleeping flowers with water, and to his surprise they began to open one by one. Ollie barked and slobbered Gabe's ankles. As the petals stretched up toward the sun, their centers started to glow. Blue at first, but then slowly changing to a smooth, creamy pink.

Strange, because that exact shade had been his mother's favorite color. He only remembered because he'd bought her a birthday present once, a leather coin purse, dyed that very same shade.

Gabe blinked again and the flowers turned a deeper red, the color of Ollie's favorite stuffed lobster. Laughing, he watched as the color turned back to ocean blue, and he thought of Gramps and how they'd always said one day they'd go swimming with the dolphins.

The color changed once more, this time to a pale, chilly white. The light glowed strongest over to Gabe's left, and he bent down to see a flat stone set in the dirt.

It was a grave.

The inscription, etched in shallow block letters, read:

WINIFRED WIST

BELOVED BY ALL WHO KNEW HER

1898–1910

MAY SHE LIVE ON WITH THE ANGELS

Once he had deciphered it, Gabe sat back on the earth, only half aware of Ollie chewing on his fingertips. Winifred must be Wynne, no doubt about it, which meant she was born in 1898. That made her over eighty years old.

No wonder she was so tired. She'd been helping people like

his gramps for nearly a century. And he knew now that she was helping, in her own way, even if it still creeped him out.

He sighed, and to his surprise his breath turned to smoke on the wind. Now that he thought about it, the air was colder than he'd expected, and was that frost clinging to the treetops in the distance? He could hardly believe that much time had passed since he'd arrived in Bone Hollow. Hadn't it still been summer when he'd left?

Prickling with curiosity, Gabe jogged toward the hilltop where Wynne had disappeared into the woods the night before, Ollie on his heels. Sure enough, not only were the treetops frosty, but a thin layer of snow covered the ground. How could that be? Just a few days ago it had been raining, chilly but definitely not snow weather.

"Time must be different here," he said to Ollie, who shrugged and decided it would be a good idea to lick between Gabe's toes. "I guess a lot of things are different here." He laughed and tried to distract Ollie with a stick, but he wasn't having it.

"Come on, boy, let's get you back before you freeze."

A bitter wind tickled Gabe's nose hairs and burned his cheeks, but it didn't hurt. Not the way it would have before. He picked Ollie up and hugged him to his chest, but Ollie didn't feel cold, either. In fact, he was still panting and wiggling his tail, despite the snow.

Back in Bone Hollow, the air was still warm, and Gabe and Ollie spent most of the afternoon exploring the gardens and waiting for Wynne to return. When the moon rose, glowing like a giant orange pumpkin in the sky, Gabe started to worry. Wynne had been so weak when she'd left. What if she was hurt and needed his help?

He searched the horizon and wasn't surprised to find several flames burning faintly over the treetops. That meant Wynne must still be hard at work. "We'll wait out here, right, boy? That way we'll see her when she comes back."

So Gabe started a fire in a small clearing not far from the cottage, and he brought out an old quilt for him and Ollie to sleep on. "She'll be home soon, now, don't you worry."

But Ollie did look worried, and Wynne didn't come back the next morning or the next night. By the third day, more flames had popped up in the distance, and Wynne still hadn't returned. Gabe was about to start walking in the direction of the nearest flame to try and find her when a pale figure emerged from behind the mist. He was wearing tiny spectacles, a long robe with no shoes, and he was bald except for two puffs of hair sticking out on either side of his head.

"You're the ghost friar. From the tunnel," Gabe said, blinking hard to make sure he wasn't seeing things.

"I prefer Brother Patrick," said the friar.

Another ghost stepped out of the mist, and Ollie bounded up to greet him, licking his fuzzy slippers and jumping on his jolly, round tummy. "Sir Carlton Stanley, cook to Her Majestic Countenance, the Duchess of Winlock."

"Former cook," said Brother Patrick. "He was sacked after two months," he whispered to Gabe. His breath was so cold, tiny icicles sprouted on Gabe's earlobe.

"What was that?" said the cook.

"No matter, *Sir* Carlton." Brother Patrick held out his hand, his expression suddenly grim. "You'd better come with us, young man. You are the new one, aren't you?"

Gabe looked from one ghost to the other. "The new what?"

"Oh dear, not the sharpest knife in the set, is he?" said Brother Patrick.

"Hush," said Sir Carlton. "He's only just arrived. We must give him some time to adjust." He turned to Gabe, talking the way you would to a three-year-old. "The new Death, dear boy. That is why you're here, isn't it?"

"Oh, no, you don't understand." Gabe stumbled back, tripping over Ollie and falling onto the soft grass. "That's Wynne's thing, not mine."

Sir Carlton and Brother Patrick exchanged a long look.

"Well," said Brother Patrick dryly. "Either way, you'd better hurry up."

Before Gabe could stop them, they each grasped one of his hands, and he was sucked up into a tunnel of swirling gray clouds, leaving Ollie behind, barking frantically at the sky. The tunnel whipped left and right, and if he looked close he saw that the gray clouds had faces. Some were screaming, some laughing, others pointing as he passed.

"Did we have to go by ghost tunnel?" Gabe shouted.

Ice pellets pelted his face. Hands reached out of nowhere, tugging on his pants and his shirt, and something wet tickled the soles of his feet. Then, as quickly as it had started, the clouds fell away and his face squelched into a mound of fresh snow.

"Where are we?" Gabe sat up, wiping the snow from his eyes. A thick layer of white covered the brick building in front of him, the cars, the trees, the softly glowing streetlights. He blinked, and saw a sign near the front of the building: Whispering Pines Retirement Village.

"Why did you bring me here?" Gabe got up, more than a little annoyed. He had snow in both ears and up his nose.

"Over this way," said Brother Patrick.

He tugged on Gabe's sleeve, and he had no choice but to follow, especially since Sir Carlton was prodding him from behind. "Hurry, hurry."

They led him to the first in a long row of single-story apartments. The pale blue door hung open. Gabe could see a lamp on inside. A siren blared in the distance, moving away from them. "What are you doing?" Gabe said as Brother Patrick slid through the open door into the room. "Someone could be in there."

"Quickly," urged Sir Carlton.

So Gabe followed, inching through the doorway into the room.

"It's empty; there's no one here."

And the small room *was* empty, apart from a bare mattress, a side table littered with used Kleenexes, and an armchair covered in plastic. On the wall, Gabe saw a picture of a thin woman with curly white hair dancing. Even though she was all alone, she looked so happy her face practically glowed.

"Why did you bring me here?" Gabe said. "If somebody's passed on, you should've called Wynne. That's her department. I—" Gabe stopped, the words getting all tangled up in his throat. Just then he saw a pair of tiny feet sticking out from the other side of the bed, wearing a familiar pair of lace-up leather boots. Wynne's boots. All the worries of the past few days came roaring back, pressing down hard on his chest.

He stepped closer, and there she was, Wynne, lying face-down on the floor, her arms and legs gray as ash.

Gabe rushed to her side and turned her over. Her eyes were open, but cold and shiny as glass. "Is she . . . ?"

Brother Patrick shook his head. "No, but we need to get her back."

"How did this happen?" Gabe said, thinking guiltily about all that time he and Ollie had wasted exploring Bone Hollow. He should have gone looking for her sooner.

"She's tired, that's all," said Brother Patrick.

"Much too tired," added Sir Carlton.

Gabe bent down and scooped Wynne into his arms. She felt even lighter than Ollie, and her bones were so thin and fragile, he didn't dare hold on too tight.

"Don't let go," said Brother Patrick, placing a hand on Gabe's shoulder.

"It'll be over in a minute," said Sir Carlton, grasping his elbow.

And then they were zooming up into the spinning clouds. None of the faces were laughing at him this time. They all watched with looks of quiet concern, and no one grabbed him or licked him or tickled his toes.

When the ride was over, Brother Patrick and Sir Carlton deposited them gently on the quilt Gabe had laid on the grass, next to the crackling fire. Ollie greeted them, but even he seemed to understand that Wynne was sick, because he didn't jump on her or attack her face with kisses.

"This is where we leave you," said Brother Patrick, bowing to Gabe. "I know you'll do the right thing."

"Until we meet again," said Sir Carlton, and then they turned around and were lost to the sea of rolling mist.

CHAPTER TWENTY-ONE
· THINGS YOU KNOW ·

Gabe sat on the blanket next to Wynne, Ollie whining in his lap. Overhead, a willow tree rattled its long branches in the breeze. He stroked Wynne's hair and touched her cheek. Her skin was hard and cold as bone.

Sitting with her like that, in the quiet of the evening, he thought all the way back to that first night, the night he'd left Macomb County for good. He could still see the fear in Miss Cleo's eyes, and the hatred on everyone's faces as they'd chased him clean out of town. Running from that anger and hate, he was certain he'd never find a place to call home again. Then, just like that, Wynne had found him and everything had changed. Maybe it had been a coincidence and maybe not, but he'd found a home, and it was all thanks to Wynne.

"Don't you go leaving me, too," Gabe said, shaking Wynne's shoulder, just a little. "You wake up, now. Go on, wake up." He shook her harder, and Ollie shifted around in his spot, whining something awful. It was bad enough that he couldn't see Gramps and Mama and Daddy, even now that he was dead. He wasn't about to go losing Wynne, too. No way.

"Come on, stop playing around." His face crumpled, the way it did right before he was about to cry, but he swallowed his tears down again. "I'm serious. I know you're an old lady, but that doesn't mean you can fall asleep whenever you want. No, sir."

He buried his head in Wynne's shoulder, and that was when he felt her stir next to him. He sat up and watched as Wynne's eyes flickered open and settled on his. Relief coursed through his veins, almost as strong as when he'd found Ollie safe and sound after that awful storm.

"That's more like it," Gabe said, laughing. He pulled her into a hug without even stopping to think about it. Sure, maybe he was hugging Death, but he didn't care.

Wynne blinked, and Ollie licked her on the mouth, but just a tiny bit. "Sorry to have caused so much trouble," she said, wheezing over each and every word. Gramps had sounded that way, back when he'd caught pneumonia, only a week or two before he passed. Gabe tried not to let that worry him. Wynne was strong, even if she wasn't young. She'd be alright.

"You didn't do anything wrong," Gabe said, and he squeezed her hand in his. He'd never held a girl's hand before, even Maisy Hughes's, on account of her complaining that Gabe sweated too much. It felt nice, even though Gabe's cheeks started to burn.

"How did I get back here?" Wynne tried to sit up, but she couldn't.

"Ghost tunnel."

"Brother Patrick and Sir Carlton?"

"Yup, that's them." Gabe shuddered a little at the memory of traveling in the tunnel, but that only made Wynne smile.

"You'll have to tell them thank you for me," Wynne said, studying Gabe's face. He wondered what she was hoping to find there.

"You can tell them yourself." He squeezed her hand tighter. "It's not like you're going anywhere."

They were quiet for a while. After a few minutes, Gabe let go of Wynne's hand and went inside to get more quilts, leaving Ollie on guard. When he returned, he covered Wynne in a thick, sparkly one tied with blue and purple ribbons, and rolled up another for her to use as a pillow.

"How about some hot chocolate?" he said. He gathered up his focus, despite Ollie pawing at his leg, and a few moments later a steaming mug of hot chocolate appeared in his hand.

"Thank you," Wynne said. She held the cup to her mouth, the steam bringing a hint of color to her cheeks. "You don't have to worry about me."

"I don't believe you."

A few more minutes passed in silence, and then Gabe lay back on the quilt, too, looking up at the stars. There was a question pressing hard against his brain, but he didn't know the right way to ask it. "So . . . how does it work? When people die, I mean . . ."

Wynne didn't answer right away. When she did, her voice was soft, like the breeze brushing against Gabe's face. "I try to help them not be afraid. That's all."

"Like with Gramps?" Gabe said, remembering that last horrible dream he'd had, where no one had come to be with him.

"Yes," Wynne said. "Like with Gramps." She took a few slow sips of hot chocolate. "How did you know I was there?"

Gabe glanced over at Wynne, who was still looking up at the sea of blinking stars. "You mean that really was you? In real life, not just in my dreams?"

"Yes, it was."

Gabe remembered how helpless he'd felt, watching Gramps suffer and fret all by his lonesome. He'd wanted so badly to reach out to him, to tell him Gran was coming soon and everything was going to be alright. "Good," he said. "I'm glad he wasn't alone." And he was. Even if his only companion had been Death.

"I guess Death isn't like I thought," he said.

Wynne tried to smile, but it quickly turned into a cough.

"You should get some sleep." He cringed at the sound rattling away in Wynne's chest. "I can help you inside if you want."

"No, I like it out here." She stared up at the stars, and he found himself wishing more than anything that she didn't see another flame. Not now, when she was so weak.

Gabe closed his eyes, and overhead the flutes played a sweet, woodsy music.

"He asked about you, you know," Wynne said, struggling just to breathe.

"Me?" Gabe sat up, trying to remember exactly what Gramps had said in his dream, but he couldn't.

"Right as I was leading him into the light, he asked who would take care of Gabe when he was gone. I told him not to worry. You have one friend who'll always be there for you."

Gabe thought surely she wasn't talking about Miss Cleo, but then he remembered Gran's words. "You mean Ollie!" He laughed. "But I don't understand. How'd you know about Ollie in the first place, way back when?"

Wynne tried to answer, but she couldn't. All that talking and laughing had sucked the breath clean out of her chest. Gabe's chest grew tight, too, like her not being able to breathe was contagious. He ached seeing her like that.

"You go to sleep, now, and that's an order," he said.

Wynne didn't say anything else. She closed her eyes, as instructed, and Gabe fell asleep to the scratchy sound of her breathing. He didn't sleep well, though, since he kept waking up to make sure Wynne was still okay. She kept on breathing through the night, though only barely.

By the next morning, Wynne was still sleeping, and two

new flames had appeared, burning over the treetops. One was buttery yellow, the other a creamy lavender, like Miss Cleo's favorite type of paint. Gabe had helped her do her whole house that color, inside and out, even Princess Carmella's miniature claw-foot bathtub. Not that he'd gotten so much as a thank-you in return.

Gabe didn't even think about waking up Wynne to tell her about the flames. He knew they belonged to people needing help, but surely the dead could wait. Only maybe they couldn't. Gabe thought of his very own gramps, scared and alone in his bed, but then he shook the thought from his head. Wynne was sick, and she needed rest bad.

At Gabe's urging, she slept all through the day and into the night. Whenever she tried to look up at the sky, to check for flames, Gabe ordered her to lie back down and close her eyes. Finally, just as the moon reached its highest point in the sky, he couldn't stop her from waking. She blinked, but didn't look strong enough yet to talk.

"How about some tea?" Gabe said, and he felt behind Wynne's ear and concentrated real hard and a cup full of steaming hot tea appeared in his hand. He brought it to Wynne's lips and helped her drink.

"You're getting better at that," Wynne said, admiring the fancy teacup Gabe had conjured from thin air. "Soon you'll be better than m—"

But Gabe shushed her and made her drink that whole cup of tea. She lay back down and didn't wake up again till the moon had been replaced by the sun. It shone soft and warm behind a row of wispy clouds.

"Time to go, sleepyhead," Wynne said, startling Gabe from his thoughts. He hadn't even seen her sit up beside him. "They need me." Her voice sounded stronger than before, but still not strong enough.

Gabe and Wynne and Ollie looked out over the treetops, where the purple flame was now beckoning, having doubled in size.

"They can wait," Gabe said, feeling Wynne's forehead. It was still cold as stone. "Besides, one of the flames already disappeared. A yellow one, just over there."

"Some people need us more than others." Wynne sat up straighter, managing a playful smile. Her skin wasn't nearly as gray as before, and her cheeks even showed the faintest hint of color. "Some people can face dying all on their own, without our help. If the light goes out like that, it means the person's already passed over."

"You need your rest," Gabe said, trying to push Wynne's shoulders back down onto the quilt.

She laughed for the first time in days. "I'm feeling better, I promise. Besides, I thought I was supposed to be the one bossing you around."

"I don't believe you," Gabe said. "And I wasn't bossing you around."

"Sounded like it to me." Wynne didn't look mad, though. If anything, her smile widened. Gabe still didn't believe her, but he didn't want to argue, either.

"It's getting bigger," she said, her sad eyes peering up at the purple flame. And it was true. Even as they watched, the ball of flame pulsed and nearly doubled again in size. "That means someone's really in need. Either they're scared or they're waiting on something."

"Something?"

"Or someone," Wynne said. She started to get up, but Gabe stopped her, and Ollie jumped in her lap just to make sure. "They need me, just like your gramps did," she said, but Gabe shook his head and pushed another cup of tea into her hands.

"They can wait one more night." He didn't know if that was true, but he couldn't stand the idea of Wynne getting hurt again. "Till you feel better."

Wynne tried to smile, but her eyes looked so sad they kept ruining the effect. She sipped her tea in silence, and Gabe lay back on the quilt, looking up at the clouds.

"One more night," she said with a sigh, and Gabe let himself sink deeper into the blanket, the tension in his shoulders and neck easing just a little.

They lay there side by side, while Ollie spun around and

around in between them, trying to get cozy. He ended up with his head on Wynne's elbow and his butt propped up on Gabe's chest.

"You're lucky to have such a good dog," Wynne said, scratching Ollie behind the ears, just the way he liked it.

"And a stinky one, too," Gabe said, but he knew what she meant. "Did you ever have a dog?"

"Pork Pie," Wynne said, eyes lighting up in the steady afternoon sun.

"Is that supposed to be a dog?" Gabe said, laughing.

"Sure he is! The best dog you ever met." Wynne paused, waggling her eyebrows at Gabe. "Well, maybe the second best."

"Dang right." Gabe was still laughing when a serious thought occurred to him. "Do you think you'll ever see him again? Pork Pie?"

Wynne thought it over, turning onto her side to face Gabe. "I hope so," she said. "But I don't really know."

"What do you mean you don't know? You are Death, aren't you?"

"That's true." Wynne managed a soft laugh, and the sound made Gabe feel warm inside. "I hold their hands, I tell them everything's going to be okay, but in the end, I don't know what happens after people die."

"But you have to know. If you don't know, who does?"

Wynne shrugged. "That's just it; I don't think anyone does.

At least not until they die. And dying, really dying, is the one thing I've never done."

"Like me?"

"Yes," Wynne said. "Like you." A wintry breeze whispered over Gabe's cheeks, and to his surprise, a few fat snowflakes drifted down from overhead. "But you still have a choice."

"I told you my answer," Gabe said. "I haven't changed my mind."

Gabe watched Wynne's face, but to his surprise her smile didn't falter. "I know."

"I mean it."

Wynne didn't say anything. Instead, she focused hard on one of the ribbon ties on the blanket, and soon a tray full of piping hot grilled cheese sandwiches appeared in her lap. "We can talk about it more later," Wynne said. "For now, eat up."

So they ate, and watched Ollie catch snowflakes on his tongue, and soon the sun had dropped below the trees again and it was dark.

Gabe rekindled the campfire, and he and Wynne spent the evening roasting marshmallows. All around, the blue flowers glowed, despite the cold, twisting around tree trunks and dangling from the branches overhead.

"Was it you?" Gabe said, staring into the crackling flames. "That night in Miss Cleo's bedroom?"

Wynne stared at the flames for a while, too, before answering. "Yes, it was me. I was your gramps."

Gabe's marshmallow turned brown and then black on the end of his stick. "But I don't understand. I saw what you did with the old man in the cemetery. You led him into the light or whatever and he disappeared. His body was there, sure, but he wasn't."

Wynne shifted uncomfortably on her rock. "Yes? What do you want to ask me, Gabe?"

"Why didn't you take me into the light, like you did with the old man?" As soon as the words were out, Gabe's throat stung, like he'd swallowed a bottle of Gramps's Christmas Day fire whiskey. He needed to know the answer, but he was afraid, too. Sure, Wynne had wanted him to be Death, just like her, but what if it was more than that? What if he wasn't good enough to go into the light, and that's why he kept on going? Why he couldn't cross over to see Mama and Daddy and Gramps?

Wynne didn't answer right away, and that stinging feeling dropped down into his chest, eating him up from the inside out.

"It's because they didn't want me, isn't it?" Gabe's belly sizzled so hot now, talking was like spewing out flames.

"Who didn't want you?" Wynne said, crunching her forehead into a frown.

"You can tell me." The heat was building up behind his eyes, too, and even though he didn't rightly know where all these dang feelings were coming from, he started to cry. "Gramps and Mama and Daddy. They didn't want to see me, did they?

That's why I'm still here? Why you had to rescue me and take me in?"

"No," Wynne said, sliding off her rock and squeezing onto his. She wrapped her arms around him and spoke gently into his ear. "What's gotten into you? Of course they want to see you. They love you, and you love them."

Gabe knew she was right, but he couldn't seem to stop crying.

"Besides," Wynne said, "you know why I didn't take you into the light, don't you?"

Wynne waited while Gabe choked out the last of his tears. They were real tears, too, the kind that dribbled down his cheeks and drenched the neck of his T-shirt. At least the snow helped some. He let it settle on his face for a while, cooling down the fire inside.

"Why?" Gabe said. "Why did you keep me?"

"I didn't keep you," Wynne said. "I just saw you. The way you help everyone around you, even when they treat you mean. No offense to your Miss Cleo. You're kind to people, and not just her, either. Your friend Niko. When she first came to Macomb County, do you remember what people said? Awful things. Talking about the color of her skin and how she'd better leave town before her family got hurt. But you didn't hear a word of that. You saw someone in need of a friend, and there you were."

"But I didn't do anything special," Gabe said. "She was better than the rest of them combined."

"Caring about people more than yourself is something special."

"Hang on," Gabe said, wiping the last of his tears from his face. "You mean you've been watching me ever since then?"

Wynne looked him straight in the eyes and nodded. He didn't know how he should feel about that, but he found it impossible to get mad. Not at Wynne.

"So you chose me?" Gabe said. "Hoping I'd take over for you when . . ."

"Not exactly," Wynne said, and Gabe was glad he didn't have to finish his sentence. "It always happens like this. When one Death goes, another's chosen. I don't know how it works, not really. Like with me and my great-gran. She didn't suspect or pray that I'd be like her when I was still alive, but when she heard about me sticking around when I was supposed to be dead and buried, she knew."

"But you were watching me before I passed."

Wynne shrugged. "I had an inkling, I guess. But I don't decide. It just is."

Gabe's lips grew numb under the coating of fresh snow. He licked them clean and scooted the tiniest bit away from Wynne. He knew she wouldn't make him do anything he didn't want to, but still.

A gust of wind shook a pile of snow from the treetops that landed smack-dab on Ollie's bottom. That sent him into a frenzy, racing circles around the campfire, barking and snarfling.

"That's some dog," Wynne said.

"Sure is." There was plenty more Gabe wanted to say and ask, but for the moment he was happy for the distraction. He didn't wanted to think any more about Death or being chosen or what his not passing over meant for his future.

"In the morning, I'm going to track down the flames," Wynne said, giving Gabe a look that meant she wouldn't take no for an answer. She stood up, refusing Gabe's help, and snuggled into the cozy pile of quilts. A few minutes later, she fell into a deep sleep, and Gabe was left staring up at the dark night sky.

There were more flames now, three in all, but the purple one was by far the brightest.

"Alright," Gabe said, draping the starry blue blanket over Wynne's tiny body. "But I'm going with you."

CHAPTER TWENTY-TWO
· THE FARMHOUSE ·

By morning, only two of the flames remained, a small red one far on the horizon, and the purple flame, so big now it seemed to tickle the belly of the sun.

"You sure you're ready for this?" Gabe said.

Wynne stood up, wobbling with the effort, and smoothed down her dress. "'Course I am." She grinned, almost like her normal self, but her eyes still looked tired. He wished he could get her to rest another day, but he knew it was no use.

"I can carry you, if you want," Gabe said, but Wynne only laughed.

"I didn't forget how to walk." She placed a hand on Gabe's shoulder. "Are *you* ready?"

Gabe let out a long breath, holding Ollie tight to his chest. "I guess. I just wish it didn't have to be ghosts," Gabe said, remembering the long, chilly tongues and groping fingers. "Couldn't we travel by portal or something, like in the movies?"

"Sorry." Wynne winked. "Ghosts are all we've got."

Gabe swallowed hard and set his jaw. "Okay, let's do this. Just don't let go of me this time."

"Promise," Wynne said. "And you don't let go of me."

Gabe closed his eyes. He didn't feel anything at first, except for an icy wind whipping around his face. Then he made the mistake of opening his eyes. Gray faces stretched past. Some smiled, some laughed, but most looked solemn and concerned. No chilly fingers reached out to grab him, and before he knew it, all the clouds cleared away and he found himself standing in the middle of a wheat field. The strands reached up to their shoulders and whispered softly in the wind.

"That wasn't half bad," Gabe said, and Wynne looked happy, too, even relieved. "I thought you weren't worried about the ghost tunnel."

"I wasn't." She folded her arms over her chest. "I was more worried about you."

"Come on, let me help you." He tried to take Wynne's arm, but she shrugged him off.

"I told you, I can walk." She smiled, and started off slowly through the brittle wheat up to an old farmhouse, the small red flame glowing in the background. Ollie raced ahead, climbing the rickety steps and barking at the open front door. Inside they found a young boy sitting on the floor next to a body. The body belonged to a middle-aged man with a short-clipped beard wearing work pants and a red flannel shirt.

The boy, who was happy enough to pet Ollie, looked up at Gabe and his eyes went wide. "Bone man," he said.

Gabe didn't know what he was talking about, but he glanced down, and just for a second his hands looked like bone, just like Wynne's on the first night they'd met.

"Maybe we should go outside," Gabe said, reaching out his bony hand. To his surprise, the boy took it, and they went out to sit on the porch, Ollie on their heels. Gabe had no idea what he was doing, but he decided for the boy's sake that he ought to try his best.

"You have a nice house here," Gabe said, hoping it was the right thing to say. "And a nice farm."

"My dad built it, the house, I mean," said the boy, fiddling with the skin on his lower lip. "But I helped. I put up the gutters all by myself. Almost."

The boy was four or five, Gabe figured, but he nodded all the same. "Is that right? I wouldn't know the first thing about putting up gutters."

"Oh, it's easy. First, you . . ."

And so the boy told him all about attaching the metal gutters to the side of the house with screws and a nail gun. Inside, Gabe could barely hear Wynne as she coaxed the man into that mysterious beyond.

"He'll be looked after, we'll make sure of it," she was saying.

"Call my sister, Florence. Her number's on the fridge. She's the only one . . . the only one . . ."

"I know," Wynne said. "We'll call her. You come with me now. Your son will be just fine."

"I need to say goodbye."

"Quickly, now."

The man stepped onto the wooden porch, though his boots didn't make a sound. "I'm gonna be gone for a while, little man. A good long while, but I'll see you again." He paused, looking to Wynne for confirmation. She chewed on her lip, too, but in the end she nodded. "You be good for your auntie Florence, you hear?"

"When will you come back?" the boy said, not looking at his dad anymore, but at the reddish-yellow light filling up the whole entire house.

"Soon, little man. I hope it'll be real soon."

He hugged his son to his chest, and then pulled him off, 'cause otherwise he probably never would have let go. With silent tears shining on his cheeks, he took Wynne's hand and walked into the light. The boy just stood there staring for a long, long time, even after the light had gone and Wynne got on the phone to call the police and leave a message for Aunt Florence.

Gabe and Ollie sat with the boy on the steps till the police arrived, and then he and Wynne and Ollie slid into the shadows.

"Bye." The boy waved, saying it over and over again.

"Who are you talking to?" said the policeman, peering into the dark.

"Bone man," said the boy, and he waved even harder.

CHAPTER TWENTY-THREE
• PURPLE FLAME •

"I don't know how you do it," Gabe said when he opened his eyes again and found himself back in Bone Hollow. "How do you know just the right thing to say?"

"I don't," Wynne said, settling down in her old spot by the fire. "I do my best. That's all anyone can do."

Gabe added one more stick to the growing flames, and then he took a seat next to Wynne. "I guess I always thought Death was different somehow. Taking Mama and Daddy and Gramps away from me. I thought Death was the same as dying, but now I know it's not."

"Everyone dies," Wynne said, smoothing a blanket over her knees and offering half to Gabe. "It isn't good or bad. It just is. It's what happens before people go that matters. They need to know that someone's there looking after them and the ones they leave behind. That's where Death comes in."

"Hmm." Gabe considered, pulling Ollie up onto his lap. "You're more like an angel, then. That's what Miss Cleo would call you."

"I hope so." Wynne covered her cheeks with her hands, but he could still tell she was blushing.

He watched her, the firelight turning her face a deep shade of orange. "How long has it been, exactly? Since you became Death, I mean?"

Wynne peered up at the stars, the slant of her cheekbone catching the moonlight. "Seventy-five years, give or take."

Gabe let out a long sigh, shaking his head. The thought of Wynne being alone in Bone Hollow for all that time made him feel like someone had grabbed his insides and wrung them out to dry. "Didn't you miss them? All the people you left behind?"

"Sure I did," she said, without taking her eyes from the stars. He could see something powerful in those eyes, even from where he was sitting. A longing so deep and old, it was bigger than the ocean. Bigger and wider, too. "But Granny showed me how she helped people, like I showed you, and I knew I couldn't say no."

Gabe sat with that information for a while, the air pressing down on him like a heavy stone lid.

"I'm tired, Gabe. Real tired." She tilted her head toward him, and he could see just what she meant. Her eyelids had turned gray and brittle at the edges, and her eyes . . . There was something so old about them, almost ancient. "I don't want to let anyone down, I don't, but I won't be able to do it for much longer."

She kept looking at him, and Gabe was too scared and

ashamed to look away. The air grew even heavier, bearing down on his chest and squeezing around his throat.

"Even us Deaths can't stick around forever." With that, she slid off the rock and curled up on the ground, pulling the quilt tight around her knees. Gabe scooted over beside her.

"You mean there's more than one of you?" A tiny hope flickered inside him. If there were others, then maybe one of them could take over for Wynne.

"Every Death has their own area. That way . . ." Wynne tried to keep going, but her voice grew hoarse and turned to a cough.

"Have you ever met one?" Gabe said once she'd recovered.

Wynne shook her head, and she looked so small and sad and lonely, Gabe couldn't stand that he was letting her down.

"How about some tea?" he said. "You need something warm, to make you feel better."

But Wynne wasn't listening anymore. Her gaze had shifted from him up to the purple flame now taking up half the sky.

"I'm afraid we don't have time for tea," she said, patting Ollie gently on the rump. "One more visit, I think, and then I can rest."

Gabe didn't like the way her words sounded so final, but he didn't have time to argue. She'd already taken his hand. "Hold on to Ollie and close your eyes. Picture the purple flame in your mind. The sweet lavender and icy pink. Imagine it's calling to you, drawing you closer and closer."

This time, Gabe felt the wind brushing gently over his cheeks. He grasped on to Ollie's fur as tightly as he could, but it was all over in a few seconds. No ghostly faces or fingers or tongues. His bare feet settled on frozen grass, and then the wind went still and Gabe opened his eyes to the sound of squawking chickens. As he looked around at where they were, a ball squeezed against the inside of his ribs, like it was trying to break out. The cool lavender paint sparkled under the light from the full moon, and the night was quiet, apart from the chickens and the roar of that bright purple flame.

CHAPTER TWENTY-FOUR

· MISS CLEO ·

"Miss Cleo," Gabe said, to Wynne and to Ollie and to no one in particular. "It can't be."

Wynne's hand tightened around his. She looked the way he would always remember her, sad and hopeful all at the same time.

"I think this one's for you," she said, so quiet he could barely hear. Her face had grown pale and sickly again, the soft skin slowly turning back into bone.

"But you were fine," Gabe said. "Back at the campfire. I was going to make you a cup of tea."

"I know." Wynne smiled, and he could tell by the way her lips quivered that it took every last ounce of effort. "Don't worry about me, not now. You have to be strong."

"I can't go in there," Gabe said, every inch of his body starting to pulse in protest. "I told you I wouldn't do it. I . . . Wynne, she can't be . . . she just can't."

Wynne squeezed his hand. It was cold and hard, and after

a moment it fell from his grasp. Wynne sank down onto the frost, like she couldn't support her own body anymore.

"But you were better! Just now. Wynne!" He grasped her by the shoulders, trying to pick her back up again, but she couldn't stay upright. "Wynne . . ."

She looked up at him, love and sadness and relief in her eyes.

"I knew you were the one," she said, though it was so quiet he had to press his ear right next to her mouth to hear the words.

"But I'm just me; I'm not anyone special. I'm not like you," Gabe said. Overhead, the flame sputtered and spit, but Gabe didn't care. "I can't leave you here."

Wynne pushed him toward the door, with the very last of her strength.

He wanted to argue, to say there was no way in hell he was leaving her alone, but then Ollie plopped down right by her side.

She opened her mouth, like she wanted to laugh, but she couldn't.

"You keep an eye on her, boy," Gabe said, tears filling up his eyes. "Just till I get back. You make sure she's okay."

Wynne blinked. "Thank you," she mouthed, though not a word came out.

Still, he didn't want to go, but the flame kept on roaring in his ears, and he knew he had to do it. For Wynne, and maybe for Miss Cleo, too.

Tearing himself away, he hurried for the door before he changed his mind. He didn't let himself think about what he might find inside. The living room smelled just the way he remembered it, full of dust and chicken feathers and Miss Cleo's greasy old toe cream. He was surprised to see his picture still sitting on the mantelpiece, in the cobbled-together frame he'd made from bits of stray wood. The TV was blasting *The Price Is Right*, Miss Cleo's favorite show.

He didn't see her at first, and a wave of relief shot through his chest, but then he took a step closer to the TV and there she was, her big blue hair poking up over the top of her worn-out green recliner.

A sticky ball pushed its way up Gabe's throat, and he was certain he'd never be able to say a single word to Miss Cleo.

Then he eased around the sofa and saw her watery eyes peering up at him. She looked so small and frail and alone that he was talking before he even knew it. "Don't be scared, now, Miss Cleo. I'm here. It's me, Gabe. I've come back home to help you."

He didn't know what he expected. Maybe for her to start hollering and calling him a monster and telling him to get the heck out of her house, or maybe the opposite. Maybe she'd hug him after all this time and finally say she was sorry. Instead, she just blinked those milky eyes at him, like she was trying to brush the cataracts right out. She scrunched up her forehead and screwed up her lips, and even though he knew he'd only been gone a few months, he swore she looked ten years older than the last time he'd seen her, her gray wrinkles drooping down her hollowed-out cheeks.

"You can come with me now, Miss Cleo. Everything's going to be alright."

But it wasn't going to be alright, because just then she pointed at him and her hand started shaking. She opened up her mouth real big, almost like she wanted to scream, but instead she said, "Dan?" She stood suddenly, leaving her body behind in the chair, and reached out for him with hands like claws. "Is it really you?"

Gabe stepped back, thinking she was having some kind of fit, but then he remembered. His eyes drifted back to the mantel and the picture next to his. It was a faded photo in a polished gold frame. The man in the photo was wearing wire-rimmed glasses and a brown corduroy suit. At the bottom was a plaque that read, "In loving memory, Daniel Scott Filner."

"Your husband?" Gabe said as Miss Cleo pulled him tight to her chest. She was shaking all over. Shaking, and sobbing, too. "No, Miss Cleo, it's—" He was about to say "me," but then he stopped. Miss Cleo had been waiting for someone, only it hadn't been him. A few months ago, that would've eaten him up inside, but now he was mostly worried about getting back to Wynne. And maybe it made sense that Miss Cleo missed her husband more than she missed him. At least she had found someone in her life to care about.

"You came back for me," Miss Cleo said again, shaking so hard he had to hold her around the waist to keep her from falling. "I knew you would. Life wasn't easy after you left. Scrounging around to pay the bills. Stuck up in this house all alone, for years. But I always said, I told 'em you'd come back for me one day, and look, you finally did." Miss Cleo took a few deep breaths and wiped the bulk of the tears from her face. She fixed Gabe with an expression he'd never seen before. Vulnerable and scared, like whatever he said meant the whole entire world to her. "You did miss me, didn't you? When you were gone?" Just then the TV went to commercial, and Gabe glimpsed his reflection in the blank screen. As he'd suspected, he wasn't Gabe anymore, but a middle-aged man in a corduroy suit.

"Of course I did."

Gabe pushed down all the old, nasty thoughts that were warring inside his head, how Miss Cleo had never missed the real him, not one tiny bit.

"I guess it's time to go," she said, staring at the ball of golden light that was blazing where the front door used to be.

"I guess so," Gabe said.

Supporting most of her weight, he helped her toward the door, but Miss Cleo stopped him halfway. She reached for the mantelpiece. He was certain she was going to pick up the photo of her husband—maybe she wanted to take it with her into the great beyond—but she didn't.

Instead, she rested a hand on his very own picture.

"Whatever happened to you?" she said, a fresh round of tears filling up her eyes. "Can't say I'll ever forgive myself for how I treated that boy. I done wrong by him, sure enough, and now he'll never know that I was sorry."

Gabe couldn't think of a single thing to say, but in the end he didn't need to.

"Do you think he could ever forgive me?" She looked deep into his eyes, and in that moment he was certain she knew. That somehow she could see him inside his body, right along-side Dan.

"I know he would." Gabe squeezed her tighter to his chest, and Miss Cleo let out a long sigh of relief.

"You were a good boy," she said in his ear, her words low and ragged and fierce. "A real good boy."

She squeezed him so tight he thought he might burst, and then all of a sudden she let him go.

"Miss Cleo, wait, you need my help."

"You already helped me," she said, walking toward the light, all on her own. Just before she left, she turned to him and smiled. "More than you know."

With that, the light grew brighter and brighter, and just when it got so bright Gabe had to shield his eyes, a crack of thunder shook the house and, with a snap, Miss Cleo, and the light, were gone.

"I knew you could do it," Wynne said when Gabe finally

came back to his senses and hurried onto the lawn. Ollie was still sitting by Wynne's side, his paws resting protectively on her lap.

"She's gone," he said. He wiped his face and found his cheeks warm and wet with tears. "Is it always like this? This hard, I mean?"

Wynne opened her mouth, but she couldn't answer. Her whole body started to shake, the same as Miss Cleo's. Gabe grasped her under both arms and helped her to her feet, but she had to lean against him to keep from falling.

"Close your eyes, now," Gabe said, taking the lead. She did, and Gabe was about to close his eyes, too, when he saw another flame flicker to life on the horizon.

This one wasn't red or purple but a faint, feathery white, and he didn't know how he knew, but he did, deep down under his skin. This flame was beckoning him back to Bone Hollow.

CHAPTER TWENTY-FIVE

· YES ·

As soon as they got back, Ollie started to whine. Gabe laid Wynne down on the quilt next to the fire, and Ollie licked her cheeks and forehead and chin.

"Quit it," Gabe said, but Ollie wouldn't listen. He lay down with his paws on her chest and kept right on licking.

Wynne lifted her hand, like she meant to pet him, but it fell back to the ground.

"You rest, now," Gabe said, pushing a loose braid out of her face. She was shifting again, between Wynne and the skeleton, but he hardly even noticed.

"Thank you," she said, but he could barely make out the words through all that shaking.

"You're gonna be fine," he said, and he was crying again, and rubbing her cheeks and hands to try and warm them up. "You don't need to thank me."

But then he saw that she wasn't looking at him, but just past his shoulder. The white flame burned in the sky over the cottage, waving to and fro in the wind.

"Why is it here?" Gabe said. "There's no one here who's going to die, it's only us. It's . . ."

She blinked, and her eyes focused again on his. "Thank you." The words whistled in her chest, and he wanted to make her stop talking, to tell her to concentrate on her breathing.

Instead, he said, "For what?"

"For being my friend. It's been so long since I've had one, I almost forgot what it was like."

Gabe choked and tears filled up his mouth. "Not just me," he said as Ollie nuzzled his nose deeper into Wynne's ribs. "Ollie, too. We're both your friends, and we always will be."

In the background, the wood flutes played a spry, lively sort of melody, but there were sad notes, too. Deep and full of longing.

"You're going to be brilliant," she said after a while, the wind blowing her hair around her face, almost like she was underwater.

"You're not leaving us." He forced her up and hugged her to his chest. "I won't let you."

She tried to smile but couldn't. "I'm tired, Gabe. So, so tired. It's time I lay down and rest."

Nearby, the flame grew, like a wave building up over their heads, getting ready to crash. "But you can't die, Wynne. You can't! You're Death. It doesn't work that way. Who will help you into the light? Who will hold your hand?"

Wynne's sad gray eyes dropped to Gabe's hand, already holding hers.

"Oh," he said, and he couldn't make any more words come out after that, partly because he saw what she meant, and partly because both of their hands, his and hers, were made of smooth, white bone.

"I don't want you to go," he said, searching her eyes, which were at one moment gray and sparkling, the next hollow. "You're my friend. Besides, I can't do it, not like you. How will I get from place to place by myself? How will I help them? How will I know what to say?"

"You'll know," she said, and then she did smile, at him and at the flame that had now swallowed the cottage and the trees and everything apart from its own cool white light.

"I'm so proud to have met you," she said, tears cutting a path down her smooth, white face. "From the moment I first saw you, I knew you would say yes." She turned away from him and stared off into the light, her smile growing stronger.

"But I need you here. I'm not like you, you're wrong. I'm selfish and lonely and I don't want to go on helping people without you."

"But you will," Wynne said, only a little of her old sadness left in her voice. She tried so hard to get up that Gabe had no choice but to help. He couldn't stand to see her struggle.

"Besides," she said, taking a shaky step toward the light, "you won't be like me. You won't be all alone."

Ollie yipped and yapped and licked Wynne's fingers, and Gabe was just about to ask what she meant when he saw it. Like that day he'd looked in the mirror at the funeral home and the first time he'd met Wynne. Ollie was dead, too, not ugly, not rotten, but just dead.

"But when? When did it happen?" Suddenly, it was like all the breath had been sucked out of his lungs.

"A branch caught him that night in the storm," Wynne said, ruffling the fur on the back of Ollie's neck. "I found him and brought him back here. It was a miracle if I ever saw one."

"So he's like me, then?"

"Like us."

"But how? How did you do it?"

Wynne laughed, a real laugh that made her bony face shine. She took another step toward the light, and it was like that white glow was filling her up with energy, bringing her back to life again. "I didn't do anything. I didn't know I'd find you until I saw you, but there you were. Plain as day. My 'yes.' And somebody must have known you couldn't stand to say goodbye to your real best friend, not for anyone or anything in the whole wide world. And so here he is, too, right by your side."

"Is that why he wouldn't eat the food at first, and then he would?" Wynne nodded, but Gabe blinked his eyes in confusion. "But . . . but, who decides? I still don't understand."

"Neither do I," she said, taking another step away from him, into the light. "It's time."

Gabe shook his head, tightening his grip on Wynne's hand. "You can't go. I won't let you."

"I thought I told you, Gabe. It's no good bossing people around." She offered him a wide grin, and her eyes took on the same familiar sparkle. He wanted to stare at that smile forever, but she wiggled her hand free from his. "My time's over now, and I'll miss you something awful. But don't you worry about me. I'm happy, Gabe, I promise. I'm ready for a good, long rest."

With that, she turned and walked slowly into the light. It was so bright it blinded him, but it was cool and shimmering and wonderful, too. Ollie barked and howled, and inside Gabe was crying out, too. Crying out for Wynne to stay.

"Goodbye, Winifred Wist," he called, tears snaking down his cheeks and dripping into his mouth. The light flared. Ollie barked harder and wiggled his bottom more than he ever had before. "Goodbye!" he said, and then he couldn't help himself.

He ran after her. He took her hand just as she was leaving, her body flickering in and out, not a skeleton anymore. Only pure white light.

"I'll miss you."

And then he kissed the second girl he'd ever kissed in his whole dang life, and the light trembled and nearly exploded, and then, with nothing but the tiniest pop, it was gone.

Gabe turned around, Ollie still barking and yipping and spinning around, chasing his own tail. He didn't know what he expected to see lying on the quilt in the place called Bone

Hollow, but what he found was nothing. Nothing apart from a tiny shimmer of silver. Gabe bent to pick it up, and found his mother's St. Christopher medal, sparkling in the firelight.

He didn't know how long he stared at it, but after a while, the tone of Ollie's barking shifted, and Gabe turned around to see a new flame burning on the horizon.

"I think that's for us," Gabe said, and the strange part was, even though the tears were still fresh on his face, he was happy, too. Because Death wasn't how he'd thought it was, and maybe life wasn't, either. And that meant that Mama and Daddy and Gramps really were okay. They hadn't been scared or alone when they'd died, Wynne would have made sure of that, and maybe, if he was lucky, they were out there somewhere, waiting for him.

As for life, the way he saw it, he'd never done anything really good when he was alive, except maybe for rescuing Ollie, but now . . . Now he had a chance to help people see Death the way he saw it. Sad, sure, but also happy and kind and vast, like the ocean he and Gramps used to imagine. A deep, endless ocean, with rushing waves and a surface that reflected back each and every star.

CHAPTER TWENTY-SIX

· EPILOGUE ·

It was snowing the day Ollie saw his first flame, burning in the quiet woods. He left Gabe sleeping on the grass and followed it.

He smelled the deer before he saw her. Sharp and musky and scared. Ollie had never been that close to a deer before, and she flinched a little when she saw him.

Maybe on instinct, or maybe thanks to some kind of magic, Ollie knew just what to do. He got real low and crawled toward the deer with his head down. He imagined he was a deer, too, sick and alone.

When he got close enough, he started licking the deer's legs and snout and rump. The deer shuddered and, little by little, started to relax. The light descended, till it was just in front of her.

Ollie nudged her on, though her bones were brittle and near about ancient for a deer. She stood, wobbling, and Ollie used his body to hold her steady.

She staggered forward, into the light, and just before she left, she turned around and fixed him with her clear brown eyes. She blinked a few times, and then snorted happily in the air, and a moment later she was gone.

＊

A few years after that, three or five or seven, it was hard to keep track, Gabe woke to find Ollie off on one of his missions. A cozy blue flame burned on the horizon, and a moment later Gabe found himself in a hospital room painted that very same shade of blue.

The room was small, just a rolling table, a sink, and a plastic bed. At first he thought the bed was empty, but then he heard someone sniffling under the covers.

"Who are you?" said a boy, peeking out from underneath. He was young, maybe four or five, and he had blond hair that fell into his eyes.

"Who are *you*?" Gabe said, leaning down by his bedside.

"My name's Simon." Simon paused, crinkling up his forehead. "You look like a fireman. Are you a fireman? They're my favorite."

"Sure am," Gabe said.

Simon nodded, thinking it over. "It's a good thing you're here," he said. "I'm scared. Firemen always know what to do when someone's scared, don't they?"

Gabe smiled. "That's right. I know just what to do." He reached behind Simon's ear and pulled out a red ball, and then another and another.

"How'd you do that?" Simon smiled despite himself.

"Wait and see." Gabe started to juggle, a few balls at first, and then a dozen, and then so many balls it looked like he was holding one endless red rainbow.

"Don't stop!" Simon laughed.

Gabe didn't stop, until a few minutes later when a woman with a tight smile and worried eyes came into the room.

"You have to stay," Simon said, and his mother blinked at him in confusion.

Gabe came back the next day, and the one after that. The flame grew a little brighter as time passed, and, one day, when it was glowing extra bright, Gabe took the boy's hand. It was so small and weak, he couldn't help but think of Wynne. He wondered where she was now, and if he'd ever see her again.

"You're smiling," said Simon.

"So are you," Gabe said.

He held Simon's hand until his mother came to sit by his side. Later that night, the light grew even brighter, so bright Gabe had to shield his eyes.

"Goodbye," Gabe said, waving at the blinding light. "Goodbye!"

And that time, like every time, it was like he was waving at Wynne. When the boy was gone, Gabe headed back to Bone Hollow, and that night, like always, Ollie was there to greet him.

ACKNOWLEDGMENTS

Creating something new is always hard and scary, at least for me. There's the joy of knowing that you're making something magical that you hope will bring more light or whimsy or laughs or chills or whatever it is into the world, but there's also the fear of opening yourself up to criticism. Failure is a very real possibility any time you do something creative and new and challenging, but try we must. And putting oneself out there creatively is so much easier when you have lovely, talented people supporting you behind the scenes.

None of my books would be possible without my wild-child/way-cooler-than-me agent, Brianne Johnson, and I thank her for her reassurance, guidance and determination. My editor, Mallory Kass, cries at my stories way more than any human being should, and her wisdom and encouragement have helped me at many points along the way. Then there are my critique partners (i.e., partners in crime) who have supported me through good and bad, laughed with me, and generally been there to share in this dream of writing stories and hopefully making the world a better, more understanding place. Thanks to Regina, Gwen, Jill, Pati, Tod, Jeannie, Jen, Sean, Ashley, and Michael (whenever he deigns to grace us with his presence ☺).

And thanks to my awesome rescue dog, Hera. She may be afraid of everything, but deep down she has a brave soul, just like Ollie.

Finally, to the readers who have contacted me to let me know that my stories made a difference to them, your words mean so much to me, and I want to thank you for sending some of your joy and kindness my way. It is greatly appreciated.

ABOUT THE AUTHOR

Kim Ventrella spends her days searching for whimsy and wonder, even in the darkest of times. She is the author of *Bone Hollow* and *Skeleton Tree*, which *Kirkus Reviews* called an "emotional roller coaster tempered by a touch of magic." She lives in Oklahoma City, where her favorite activities include writing stories, working at a haunted house, and racing her dog in the rain.

DON'T MISS THE FIRST MAGICAL ADVENTURE FROM KIM VENTRELLA!

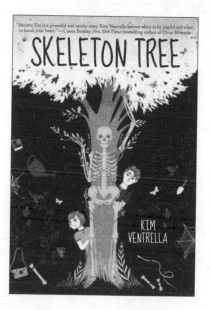

Twelve-year-old Stanly knows the bones growing in his yard are a little weird, but that's okay, because now he'll have the *perfect* photo to submit for a photography competition. But when his little sister, Miren, grows sick, Stanly suspects that the skeleton is responsible and does everything in his power to drive the creature away. However, Miren is desperate not to lose her new friend, forcing Stanly to question everything he's ever believed about life, love, and the mysterious forces that connect us.